T0156829

Never Lie Down

J. Carol Goodman

iUniverse, Inc.
Bloomington

NEVER LIE DOWN

iUniverse books may be ordered through booksellers or by contacting:

iUniverse
1663 Liberty Drive
Bloomington, IN 47403
www.iuniverse.com
1-800-Authors (1-800-288-4677)

Because of the dynamic nature of the Internet, any Web addresses or links contained in this book may have changed since publication and may no longer be valid. This is a work of fiction. All of the characters, names, incidents, organizations, and dialogue in this novel are either the products of the author's imagination or are used fictitiously.

ISBN: 978-1-4502-5543-1 (pbk)
ISBN: 978-1-4502-5544-8 (ebk)

Printed in the United States of America

iUniverse rev. date: 1/11/11

Many thanks to the Dodge Foundation, the New Jersey Council on the Arts and for fellowships from Yaddo, MacDowell, Virginia Center for the Creative Arts and Banff Center for the Arts.

For Ted, our children and grandchildren

In Memory of my parents and my sister

CHAPTER 1

*G*lorybe screamed. The black vehicle nearly knocked us over as we crossed the street.

"A hearse," I screamed back.

"Who's in there?" She panted at her escape.

"Strickland who got murdered, I bet."

Locking arms we sang, *"When the hearse goes by you may be the next to die."*

We giggled our way through town, having no idea at age twelve that this was the beginning of fear and the reality of fear… Fear for our friends, the Johnsons, and fear for Glorybe's father, the Indian, whose name I never learned and with whom I was in love.

We were almost to the river, which ran throughout our town. At Inman Avenue it bumped out like a boa constrictor swallowing a rabbit. From there it turned into Peter's Bend where the Johnsons and the other Colored People lived. Then the river flowed straight and flat under the railroad. It passed the tramps' shacks made of scrap wood and tin and on past the truck farmers that surrounded our town. The farmers gave the tramps vegetables that were going bad and let us get vegetables cheap if we picked our own tomatoes and dug our own potatoes.

"I was born in a hearse," I said.

"Oh sure you were." Glorybe pulled my pigtail.

"What do you bet I was born in a hearse?"

"Nothing."

"What'll you give me if I tell you how come?"

"How about my all-day sucker." She looked at me sideways.

"Great, the one full of pocket grit from your shorts."

Now we were high up on the river bank where there weren't any houses, just before the Rahway River runs to Perth Amboy and stretches football-field wide and deep enough for rich people's motorboats. There it becomes smooth and dark as it rolls toward the Atlantic Ocean.

We didn't have to take our shoes off. We were always barefoot unless our parents caught us. As we climbed down into the river the rocks jabbed our feet which weren't as tough as at the end of summer. But the icy water felt good on our burning feet. We climbed up the bank.

"You go," I said. I loved making her do things first because she hung back

"No, you go."

What flashed in my mind again was that this was near where they found the murdered man.

Glorybe stood at the edge chewing her lip before she set her behind on the muddy edge. I gave her a big shove. She screamed as she slid, her long blond hair flying out like feathers. Her father claimed to be the son of Chief Scarecrow, but her mother was

2

Finnish. Glorybe had outlandish big feet. That and her hair were the only things like her mother, thank God.

She hit the water. I slid down and banged right into her.

Nothing stopped us. We could do this all morning, all summer. Two slimy goopy seals, wet and muddy, the ends of her hair had turned brown like the color of my pigtails. We spread out on the grass as the sun covered us and warmed our bellies. That warmth was one of my first feelings of arousal, a hand brushing softly over me, down the insides of my legs, sighing out my breath.

So what, I thought, that Strickland was killed near here. He was killed at night. Glorybe ran a piece of grass through her teeth as she closed her eyes. Nothing ever went wrong while we were lying in the sun like that. And as a child you think nothing will ever change. The Depression seemed as far away as a foghorn you could hardly hear and the murder was as removed as a radio mystery.

"I won't go with you to look for crayfish unless you tell me how come you got born in a hearse," Glorybe announced.

I knew she didn't mean it. We went everywhere together. "You know Gruber?"

"Yeah."

"It was Gruber's hearse."

"Yeah?"

"There was a snowstorm."

"Yeah?"

"Stop saying yeah. Mom couldn't find Dad. The usual. He was out saving somebody's soul. And I wasn't supposed to get born for two whole weeks. But you know how I hate waiting."

"So she calls an *undertaker*?"

3

"Preachers and undertakers have a deal. It's good for business."

"What kind of a deal?"

"When somebody drops dead Dad calls Gruber. He does the best embalming in town. Then when Gruber gets a dead guy who has no church he calls Dad. He does the best prayers in town."

"But Gruber has a car," Glorybe said, suspicious-like.

"His car is busted. The snowstorm is coming in fast and furious. So he runs across the street to Beaucage to borrow his car but he isn't home. Then he runs to Price's, but only Richard, the kid, is home. Then he runs..."

"So the only thing left was the hearse?"

"Gruber roars it into our driveway, lifts Mom up and through that wide door, helps her lie down, you know, right on the bench where they lay the caskets, beside all those pleated black curtains, and drives through the storm to the hospital in Newark."

"Six blocks from the hospital, guess what? A noise, a bellow, a roar...an EXPLOSION. Me rocketing straight out, landing on this earth with the speed of lightning."

"Sure," Glorybe said, blinking her blue eyes.

But Glorybe knew I never lied to her, like for real. She wanted to pretend that I did so that she could show me she wasn't just under my spell. She pursed her lips. She tickled my chin with a piece of grass. "In other words you were born dead."

I kicked her foot and rolled over on my belly. We lay still in the high sun.

Before we headed for the other side of town, where we hoped the crayfish were more plentiful, I looked once more at the river, thinking I couldn't believe that a man I was acquainted with was murdered. I never knew a person who got murdered before.

I shivered as the event became more real, the event that would affect us more than I dreamed of.

The mud was drying on us. The bottoms of our feet were black as sin. We didn't care as we ran under the rusty girders of the railroad bridge and held our ears. The WPA men were jack hammering up trolley tracks. We walked slowly past the factory where The Indian worked. On top was a box as big as a car with the word in yellow letters, "*Wheatena*," a disgusting-tasting cereal. That was where Strickland had been The Indian's boss and his yard was also where our Colored friend Jeremiah Johnson worked.

"Bet you never personally seen a dead person. At her church Bess-the-Mess gets to stare directly into the corpse's face. Isn't that neat?" I asked.

"I saw Strickland following Jeremiah around in his yard yelling at him for not cutting the bushes the way he wanted. The Indian," (she also called her father The Indian) "didn't like Strickland. Nobody at the factory did. I hope they find out soon who murdered him. I don't like to think a murderer crawling in my window."

"Like the Lindbergh baby."

"My mom says we don't have enough money for somebody to snatch me."

CHAPTER 2

"*W*ant to help us fish?" Selina said. She was one of Jeremiah Johnson and Easter's kids. She was sitting on a rock in the river with a fishing pole she'd made out of a Willow branch.

"Thanks, not today, we're Crayfishing," I answered.

"Yuk, rocks are so slimy when you pick them up," Selina called.

Selina and I were always getting caught sneaking notes to each other in class. Her brother Eliah was in eight grade, two years ahead of us. He was cute except he chewed his fingernails. Sometimes they came up to my house when their father visited mine. Jeremiah and Dad talked about the Bible, what this verse or that meant. But the Johnsons didn't go to our church. They attended the Baptist church for Colored people where they hooted and sang and danced, running up and down the aisles. I told Glorybe, "In our church you have to sit so still you turn to stone in two seconds flat."

One reason Dad and Jeremiah were good friends is they were both from the south and they used words I had never heard of like, oh shucks. I didn't realize how unusual it was in those days for White people to have Colored friends until I was older. Of course children could be friends up to a point, up to maybe high school. Then Colored kids took their *place*.

My father and Jeremiah loved just plain gossip too and I loved to listen. Although they said it wasn't gossip, just trying to understand the inside workings of people, I knew better and longed for juicy stuff, but they were careful when I was around.

We were turning over the rocks in the river when I saw Jeremiah walking toward his house. I wondered what he was doing home. He worked as a handy man and sometimes yard man around the neighborhood as well as at Strickland's.

The Johnsons rented their crumbling house, which their landlord ignored. Jeremiah tried to shore up things but he couldn't do much without money. That day he was dressed up in his worn Sunday black suit.

"What you dressed up for?" I asked.

"Mr. Strickland's funeral?" Glorybe asked.

"Yes."

"Who killed him?" I asked.

"Don't know." He frowned.

"I've never seen a dead man," I said.

"I hope you never will, little one."

A yummy smell filled my nose. I turned around. Easter was holding out a plate of steaming corn bread right under our noses. She was proper as they come and brought us each a napkin. "Look at you. Carousing up the river again." She watched Glorybe and me gobble the corn bread and called out to Selina and Eliah to come get some.

Easter was the lightest in the family. Mom called her elegant because every day she dressed up with style, putting leftover clothes together, taking out the worn parts, attaching this and that, like a colorful patchwork quilt. When our church had second-hand clothing sales Mom sifted through to pilfer some for the Johnsons, even though every piece was supposedly to earn money for our church. Dad of course didn't know. Mom had her own ways of doing what she thought were right.

Selina was also light with reddish hair and taller than me. She could move quick as a sparrow. Eliah was pear color, almost yellow and with a long neck and large head and wide eyes flecked with yellow. I thought he was gorgeous.

But Jeremiah was so black you couldn't find any white to his eyes, like the inside of sunflowers. He was tall and thin and Easter cut his hair as tightly as our lawn he mowed.

"Look at you girls full of mud," Eliah said. "You're so dark you'd probably eat catfish like us." Eliah came out of the river and laughed and laughed at us, slapping his thighs. He could be shy with others but he knew us too well. And Selina, who mostly refused to copy her older brother, chimed right in behind him.

"Okay, okay." I washed myself as best I could in the river and Glorybe did too.

"If I go home like this I'll get beat up," she said.

"The Indian raise your hide?" Selina asked.

"My mom. Look at this." Glorybe held her arm close to our eyes. "She thumped me with a fork."

Seeing the scar made my feet curl with what her pain must have been. But she didn't seem intimidated by her mother.

"Worse," she said, "sometimes my mother slaps me with gooey dish-water hands."

"Uhhh," we yelped. "Much worse."

"Glorybe, stay still as a log... bend, slow. Real important we get a lot of crayfish."

She started to ask me why, again, but knew better. She understood I didn't want her to say no. She didn't know it was because I couldn't wait to see The Indian. "Strike fast," I said.

She rolled her body into a C.

"But they skitter. And I can't see them when their millions of little legs stir up clouds of silt."

Eliah was the one who showed me how to catch them. He tried to show Selina but she liked fishing better. Selina had a mind of her own. She stayed after school once because she refused to go out at recess. She didn't own boots and it was snowing. I liked her stubbornness a lot.

"Glorybe, you caught one," I screamed. By noon we had five, well, we had six. One slithered away.

"Look what I caught," Eliah called as he held up a catfish with long black whiskers. He and Selina ran to the house with the fish. I couldn't imagine eating such a creature.

We waded to the big rock and I pulled out my penknife. Mom gave it to me for my birthday. Dad didn't want me to have it. He thought it was too hazardous.

He thought things over and was more cautious than my mother, that's why it was good to have her on my side.

I laid the crayfish down on the rock, whacked their heads off, one at a time. Glorybe screamed. I screamed too when I severed the last one.

On the way home we stopped at the old largest maple in the woods. "I'll start to carve," I said. "You can finish our names." I carved 1936.

"I want to go home. I have to pee," Glorybe said.

"Go farther in the woods."

"Snakes."

"When have you ever seen a snake in New Jersey?"

"The Indian has seen plenty," she said.

"But Indians aren't scared of snakes."

"Well, I'm only part Indian."

She high-stepped it into the thicket. She always ended up brave. That's what I loved about her. When she came back I had already carved, "Theodora and Gloria."

"Why did they name you Theodora?"

"'Cause, I'm their marvelous, wonderful, adorable, lovely, sweet, smart, kid and Theodora means gift of God."

She stuck her tongue way out at me. "At least your name isn't Gloria Beatrice."

I was ecstatic we had an excuse to go to Glorybe's house. It was Saturday and her father would be home. But a heaviness of anxiety spilled into my heart and my breathing. Was I brave enough to go see The Indian and hand him the crayfish? Yet my longing was worse than longing for Christmas.

"Uh, oh, Miss Collier." She was coming toward us with her silly umbrella she held over her head, sun or rain.

"Run for it."

"Why doesn't she like you?" Glorybe whispered.

"I refuse to clean my fingernails."

"You're kidding."

"So she won't give me her stupid piano lessons anymore."

"Was your Dad mad?"

He said, "'Well I have to tell you, Theodora, God doesn't let grubby fingernails into heaven.'"

"He's a good kidder. But he wasn't even mad?"

"He gets mad at different things."

"Like?"

"If I say a dirty word."

"Like what?"

"Like shit."

"You said that out loud?"

"Everybody does it, why shouldn't I say it?"

"The Indian goes nuts if I make noise chewing my food. He stands up and bangs his fist on the table. 'I come from the prairie, where there's silence in all directions.' But sometimes I wonder if he really did come from the prairie. I have just one picture of him as a kid with a cowboy hat but he's standing on a sidewalk in Jersey City."

"Didn't you ask him?"

"He didn't answer. Just says, oh yeah, my cowboy hat."

I didn't want to think of him as a cowboy. I said, "He's an Indian."

Glorybe lived across the street from me where run down houses clustered in a block, but not as run down as the Johnson's. Glorybe's street was in back of our yard. Our yard ran from one street to the next where sat the church and our manse. In the street in front of our house stood more elegant houses and was where the Stricklands live.

We climbed the steps to Glorybe's porch, which her landlord never mended. The floor was pretty rotten and some boards were missing so you had to walk carefully. Glorybe's brother broke his foot falling into one late at night. He was six years older than Glorybe and looking back I think, drunk.

I had taken my braids out and my hair had ripples of waves and I bit my lips to make them look redder. The idea of seeing *him* was making my ankles as weak as when I tried to ice skate.

He mostly slept on his day off from the *Wheatena* factory. Glorybe always said whenever he was mentioned, "It's lucky he still has a job but he is worried. Lots of people don't have jobs but some people still eat *Wheatena.*"

When her father was awake he didn't do anything. He usually sat in the porch hammock, looking marvelous. He had hair blacker than our maid, Suzy, and as black as the hearse, I thought…but didn't want to. Glorybe's and his nose were exactly alike, long and sharp with a walnut size bump in the middle.

"Why does he keep the pipe in his mouth but doesn't light it?"

"It's just a peace pipe," Glorybe said, "He's waiting, I guess, for a war."

"Suzy thinks one is going to come in Europe so maybe we'll get to see him light it then."

"Maybe," Glorybe said. She couldn't predict her father.

He wasn't on the porch. She said something then that worried me. "He doesn't feel well." I glimpsed a great tall shadow behind the screen door and out walked The Indian. "He better not lose his job."

"How's my papooses?" His face was always the same so you couldn't tell if he were teasing or not. But I had no control over mine as it flamed up.

"You headed for a pow-wow?"

"I…we brought you a present."

"And what is that?"

I opened my hand and put three of the five crayfish in his long right palm where my thumb actually grazed his.

"Thanks so much. Gloria, take them in to your mother." When she left he looked straight into my eyes.

Don't fall over, I cautioned myself. "Could I see your jewelry?"
I choked out.

"I don't know, it's sacred."

Glorybe didn't know when he was serious either. Sometimes
he gave her a whack when she thought he was just kidding.

"Oh," I mouthed and stared at my feet.

"One reason he loves to dress up in jewelry," Glorybe had
said, "is because he hadn't been raised with other Indians."

"My Dad loves to dress up in his preacher's robes, but most
of all in his morning suit for funerals."

When The Indian was off work he wore heavy blue jeans and
an open shirt and pointy cowboy boots that were buffed to a
shine. "When you going to dance for us?" I asked.

"When you going to bring me feathers? Eleven's the number
and no chicken feathers, Theodora, minister's kid." That's what
he always called me, which made me blush again, like a minister's
kid was something mysterious and exotic instead of the way the
congregation wanted me to be, a bland goody-goody.

Then he shut his eyes. That meant I should leave him alone in
the hammock. He didn't talk much anyway. But I stood another
minute to take the image of his face away with me, those deep
lines on either side of his narrow lips, like lines that Indians paint
on their faces. His forehead was rugged as a rock cliff, high and
broad and curved outward. His shut eyelids were round and
smooth as river stones. His ears were tucked way back as if the
wind had blown them. I wanted so much to touch his face.

"Did he ever have a horse?" I once asked.

"Not that I know of," Glorybe said.

Often when I was about to sleep I thought about him on the
prairie. I saw him with just a little leather piece in the front of him
and the rest of him naked and his skin the color of moccasins,

and his hair falling down his back in a great thick braid and I was Princess Pocahontas and he took my hand and led me along the river where it widened and smelled sweet until we came to his tepee, covered with bear skins and birch bark. The tepee was giant and as impressive as our church or maybe more like a great cathedral. I belonged there with him and he cooked me coyote meat over hot coals and the singing sound of the river lullabied us to sleep.

CHAPTER 3

*W*hen I handed the two remaining crayfish to my mother she looked distracted. She walked with them to the kitchen. When she looked like that I always assumed she was thinking of her next move. But I didn't think about this as odd, which was unheard of for those times. She fought for equal rights for Colored people. I didn't understand her insistence on improving their lives. Not until years later, when I was grown, did she explain her fervent urgency, which had come from something horrible that happened in her childhood.

But when my mother married my father she had no idea of their differences. My whole life they said they weren't fighting or even arguing. They called it discussing. Mostly that was true except for their approaches, which crowded up their faces in an erupting storm. I can hear my father's booming voice quoting the Bible "If you believe you, can move mountains."

"That's not enough," my mother screamed back. "We have to take a shovel and dig away the mountains."

Our house was set back from Church Street because the church and manse were on about an acre and a half. On one side of our manse was the church but on the other side was a wooden fence where stood *The House*. That's what my parents called it. Mrs. Brown lived there. She had red cheeks and a barrel stomach and her hair combed, just so, to hide her bald spot. I liked her a lot. When I was little she handed me cookies over the fence and knit me doll blankets. At the time I had no idea why my father and mother disapproved of her and why my father sighed and said if only she would see her way to the straight and narrow. Every once and a while he tried to get her to join our church. "I'm not a joiner" was her answer.

A bunch of young women lived with her and she called them the cousins. I wondered why they didn't resemble one another in the slightest. They dressed in silky colors and lazed around all day long and at night men visited them. I thought they were very popular.

"How come you got the smallest bedroom?" Glorybe had asked.

"I like it. I can see the cousins anytime. I can look over at Gruber's and see the caskets coming and going and I can hear the choir practicing in the church. Anyway, Annie came first."

Even though my sister had the best room she crabbed. She crabbed when the sun shone, or when our maid, Suzy, served her her favorite dessert, baked Alaska...that it wasn't often enough. She crabbed when she played the piano really well and she even crabbed when she got an A on her term paper because it wasn't

A+. She was queen of the roost. Even I thought she was queen of the roost.

Next year when she would be seventeen she could drive and then she was going to go to college. I hated her going away. Partly I liked her crabbing which made me seem like an angel. She told me I couldn't have her room anyway because it was still her room and she said she was going to screw on a hasp and a combination lock. She knew, of course, I'd snoop. What she didn't know was that I would unscrew the hasp.

Dad sort of staggered out of his study looking blank. That was because Saturday was sermon-writing time. All week he'd jot his thoughts on scraps of paper and leave them around the house. Come Saturday he'd give Annie and me a nickel to find them. Annie long ago refused so I got two nickels. My mother said his hunting came from his farm-boy days, having to track down where the chickens dropped their eggs.

Dad's wavy white hair was mussed. He mussed it when he was thinking. His white shirtsleeves were rolled way up his big arms. He had the biggest hands of anybody I knew and hair as soft as baby chicks grew on them. When he took my hand his grip made me think he could lift me up by his pinky. Tall and athletic he still looked like the basketball star that he was in college.

In the winter when I finished my homework he would say, "Theodora, let's hoop it up." We would run across our yard to the church's community house gym.

"Wonderful, sweetpeas," Dad said about the crayfish. "My little water rats, spending more time in the river then in church." I looked at Glorybe and grinned. I had plans for going to church soon as we could to look for pigeon feathers so The Indian would dance, not exactly the kind of going to church that Dad meant.

"I gotta go," Glorybe said. She ran home.

"Dad, did you conduct Mr. Strickland's funeral?"

"Yes, I did."

"Who killed him?"

"We don't know yet."

I shivered and decided then I would never go to that part of the river again.

CHAPTER 4

When I woke the next day thinking of murder, which used to happen in another place, another country, or another time in history, I felt a horrible reality had been kept from me and that murder was everywhere and surrounding me. I jumped out of bed hoping sunshine would make me feel better.

It was Sunday and we had a tradition of walking in the cemetery and then the park. I was glad to be going to the cemetery. Dad promised to show me Strickland's grave. I wanted to be sure he was dead.

But at the gate of the cemetery my mother left and we met her later in the park. When I asked her why she didn't come with us her remark was, "Who wants to look at a lot of dead people? I believe in here and now."

She also didn't attend funerals.

Annie said, "Then nobody will come to yours."

"But I won't know, will I?"

We all laughed.

Lately Annie didn't come. She said she was too old for walking. When I was younger Annie taught me the best places to pee, where gravestones were tall enough to hide us. Now Annie would deny she ever did such a thing. Queens don't pee. She even locks the bathroom door. Sometimes I felt she had already moved away from us and her empty room was as silent as dead air.

That day she took off her silk crepe dress, (aunt Florence's hand-me-down) her green hat with yellow water lilies and blue half veil, and her stockings that she'd spent eons fiddling with to get her seams straight.

Annie said she would rather read. But I knew she was going to walk to the baseball field with one of her girl friends and hang around, wetting her lips and sticking her grinning, flirting teeth out toward the boys. I was disgusted. And I craved to be her.

Even though my mother was only a foot taller than our kitchen sink she could sure walk fast in tiny steps. She had removed her Sunday hat so her Titian hair blew wildly in the strong wind, looking as if some grasses were coming untethered. My father's hair was the opposite, waves as neat as a permanent except when he was writing his sermons and messing it up. When he washed it he put on the stocking cap my mother had made him out of a worn silk stocking, keeping the top, cutting it and knotting the frayed ends, making him look Japanese with a top knot.

Dad and I strolled toward the new graves on the hill above the park. "Why do you love the cemetery?" I asked.

"Well, let's see, so I can say, *hi* to all the people I buried."

"But they're dead."

"True but I'm honoring their time on earth."

That didn't quite make sense but I was still at the age where a lot of grown-up ideas didn't make sense.

"This one is Lambert Soul, remember him, Theodora?"

"The guy that sat in the back in church and snored?"

"Yep. He worked at the Union Bank before the banks lost peoples' money. Now his wife sells that bread that we buy to help her out."

"But it crumbles like sawdust. I caught Mom scattering some to the squirrels."

Dad smiled uncomfortably.

At the next grave marked by an impressive polished granite stone, I said, "What did Henry Tuttle die of?" This was the part I loved the most, his telling what people died of.

"Melancholia. A kind of mental illness. He sat on his porch with his head down."

When were we going to get to Strickland's grave? I wiggled. Dad wiped the corner of his eyes under his glasses. I was so glad nobody was around. But he never seemed to care who saw him roll out the tears. Annie and I once went to the movies with him and we were so embarrassed walking out as he dabbed his eyes that we ran ahead.

There was a new grave in front of us. I caught my breath. "Is that where he is buried?" I asked, looking at the soft dirt in shape of a coffin. I envisioned his bleeding body was nourishing the sprouts. My toes grew numb like when a spook jumps out at you on Halloween.

"Yep, Mr. Strickland's grave," Dad said.

I stared waiting, ready for the unexpected, like my father's story of a corpse tied down in the open casket at Gruber's. He was tied down because he had been nearly doubled over with arthritis. In the middle of the parade of people walking by to view the body the guy suddenly sat up, the bonds having broken, and the whole room cleared, stumbling into one another, gasping. I felt that somehow Strickland's ghost was going to jump out or haunt me and actually that turned out to be true.

"Was Strickland a really bad guy?"

"People are not all one thing," Dad said. "Once I saw him buy ice cream for a group of kids."

"Really?" Dad started to stroll again, and although I wanted to look some more, I followed.

We were nearly to the end by the high stone wall. "Why do you sing when you're getting dressed for funerals?"

"Because I'm glad to be burying the people."

"Daddy," I screeched. "That's weird."

"Most people were miserable, sick, before the Lord took them and they will be going to a better place."

"All of them?"

"I'm optimistic." He flipped my pigtail.

"You sing while getting dressed but then why do you cry when you're conducting the funeral?"

"Because I'll miss them too."

We were about to turn the corner where we stopped at my brother's grave. Once a year in April my mother went with us to his grave after we picked violets along the river to lay on his stone. We had also planted violets there. His grave was marked with a small flat stone and mossy letters, which Dad quickly scraped off with a stick.

John Logan Davis
Born April 6, 1914, died April 8 1914

I thought about him a lot. John would be in college already. Would he look like Dad? Would he smoke a pipe, like Glorybe's Dad? Maybe he'd have a girl friend who'd be nicer to me than

Annie. But how could I be missing so badly somebody I'd never even said hello to?

"Did you go to John's funeral?" I had asked my mother.

"I went to the service. I just couldn't go to John's grave for a year and I even hate to go now."

That was the moment I learned that sadness could last one's lifetime. I had thought that grown ups were strong enough to push those feelings away. That was the first time I thought about my mother and father losing John. I had only thought about me being cheated out of a brother.

"I don't remember the first time I saw his grave," I said.

"You were only three," Dad said. "You helped us pick the violets. You pulled up the roots because your fingers were too young to snip the stems and that's when we decided to plant them."

CHAPTER 5

$\mathcal{B}$ack to the gate and over to the park to meet Mother. She was near where once we saw a man, Glorybe and I, lying on top of a woman. It looked so funny. I told Suzy afterwards. She said, "Some men like to use ladies for pillows."

"Why don't ladies use men?"

"Men have sharp hip-bones."

I was having trouble, something was wrong with the new dress Mom had made me. I could feel it pulling loose at the waist. She never left enough material because she bought less than the pattern called for to save money. Last year, the top of my left sleeve had pulled all the way loose in school. Then she gave me pins to carry in my book bag and said, "you better start wearing underwear to school, Sweetpea; you never can tell what might give way next."

But of course I didn't wear any. I loved the breezes up my skirts too much.

We met Mom and started home. That's when I asked, "Why are the gates to the cemetery rusty?"

"The truth is," Dad said, "The church doesn't have money enough to paint them in these bad times."

"Why can't the WPA do it? They work on the park."

"The park is government property and those are government workers. The cemetery belongs to our church."

"There is a big separation between church and state," Mother had explained with sarcasm.

"Don't you really think there should be, Weebeth?" Dad asked.

"You know I think that sometimes the church should jump into muck and mud of the real world and shout at bad government."

"Is the church ever wrong?" I asked, astonished.

"The church is just people," Mom said, "And people sitting in the pews are just as bad as people sitting on bar stools."

"Well, let's hope we have a little good influence," Dad said, sharply. But she smiled nicely at him, letting him know she believed in him, yet that he wasn't going far enough for her. The tension in her voice was the clue of her gearing up for her Colored peoples reform committee.

A few months back Mom said to Glorybe and me, "Good. You girls come see what goes on in this town."

And seeing what happened thoroughly influenced me that summer.

Joining her was Easter, Lilia Hunt who was also Colored and Mom's best friend Margaret Dean who was White. The ladies marched to the YMCA down on Main Street, in the door and up to the desk.

Easter said, "I'd like to register my son Eliah." She had a way of making her whole face look as inspired as Joan-of-Arc. It's like her words dressed up her whole face.

The man behind the desk looked like a kid himself. He had odd streaks in his eyes, like a cat's. His Adam's apple yo-yoed in his throat. "We're really sorry but we're full up."

Mom moved in, her arms crossed over her chest. She put on her deeper southern accent. "That is less than the truth, mister. I came here yesterday and you said I could not only register my husband but anybody else I knew since membership was way down because of the Depression. So now these ladies want to sign up their boys." She pointed to Easter and Lilia.

"But..." the man was flustered.

Mom laid her hands flat-out on the desk and was leaning toward him. She tapped her feet.

The man's Adam's apple lay still as a pebble. "It's expensive. These people can't afford the Y."

"Oh, these people," Mom said. "How do you know what they have? They happen to have plenty of money"

I was fascinated how Mom could lie. I was glad Dad didn't hear her. He despised lying.

"There just isn't room, ma'am."

"Call the manager, please."

"He's out of town."

She signaled all of us to follow her down the hall. The young man scooted around the desk. "Wait. You can't go there. It's private. Come back here."

Mom paid no attention and dashed on, the caravan behind her. She knocked on the manager's door. By golly the manager was there. Easter pursed her lips at Mom and Mom smiled. The manager with blond curly hair leaned backwards. When Mom told him the encounter he nodded but I could tell he had never heard anything like this his whole life. Colored people wanting to join the Y.

Mom put her hands on her hips. She was calm and cocky and charming all in one.

"Sorry," he said, That's impossible."

"Why is that?"

"We just can't accommodate everyone."

"What does the initials YMCA mean?" Mom asked.

"Young Men's Christian Association."

"Jesus said, Do unto others as you would have them do unto you."

"That has nothing to do with it. This is an organization."

Mom laughed with sarcasm. "Well we're going to stand here until you say your prejudice out loud, until you say what you shouldn't."

"Go ahead and stand there all you want." He stood up, turned and walked through a door with the words *bathroom* on it. We stayed a little longer but when he didn't come out Mom started back down the hall again. We followed and in the lobby she shouted, with all the people listening, "Young Men's Christian Association. Don't you believe it."

When we left Mom and her friends' heads were high as they pounded down the sidewalk, like this was the beginning of a war.

CHAPTER 6

"Today's the day," I told Glorybe. "The Indian will dance." And later this would be important as the Depression continued.

We climbed the steps softly to her room with dim stained wallpaper of faded roses. Her rug had once been bright pink but was also stained from a long ago dog of the landlord's. Just about everything belonged to the landlord.

She rummaged through the top drawer and found her dark glasses, to look like a movie star. We were going to skip out fast because we were afraid of seeing her mother. She looked us over, sniffed us out, always ashamed of us. No sneakers, dirt on our necks, ice cream left on the corners of our mouths.

But I never saw her out of her apron, or the curlers out of her hair. Even when she went to the butcher. And I never heard her say a nice word.

"Where's your dad?" I asked Glorybe, hoping to snatch a glimpse.

"Got me. Sometimes he doesn't feel good."

"Why?"

"We don't know."

I worried. "Maybe dancing will make him feel better."

We sneaked away without her mother noticing. She was in the living room drinking a coke.

She drank a lot of coke and put something in it so it wasn't flat. She was listening to the radio, which was bigger than ours, a real piece of furniture; snap the doors open, fold them back and lo-and-behold the radio with a cloth hiding the speaker.

We were across the lawn to the church when Glorybe stopped, "I don't know... Weiggle."

"Don't worry. First we look through the windows to see if he's around."

Glorybe pursed her lips.

"Give it up. We will be sure Weiggle isn't lurking." He was the janitor of our church and we both were frightened of his anger. Once he nearly hit us with his mop, just because we were playing tag, jumping over the pews.

He wasn't in the Sunday school rooms or the assembly room. Not down in the gym. Sometimes Daddy told older kids, not just from our church, they could play basketball there on rainy days.

"But how come you get to play with them?" Glorybe asked.

"Last winter I gave those guys the word. I crossed my arms over my chest and called out, 'My Dad owns this church. Sooooo, you have to let me play with you.'"

"You didn't!"

"At first they paid no attention."

"A girl and a squirt." Glorybe laughed.

"But when Dad heard about that he was good and mad. Even tried his stern look bit. But you know he's mostly talk and no action."

"So how come you got to play?" We were still peering in all the windows of the community house part of the church. "Dad said, 'Theodora, I don't own the church and don't you ever say that again. Everyone in the congregation owns the church.' So I went back and said to those big guys, 'My Dad doesn't own the church, I do, so you gotta let me play."

They made faces and kept on dribbling the ball. One of them laughed. But the one with glasses said, 'Okay kid, you can be on my team.' I almost fainted. Then they almost fainted because Dad had taught me and I played really good."

"There he is," I whispered. Made my heart go rubber-dub-dub. Weiggle never washed the windows of his tool room where he hung around, smoking his disgusting cigar, his two shaggy dogs lying next to his chair, stinking up the place and sometimes pooping. He wore his same old gray lederhosen, his polio leg up on the desk. But when he shoveled in coal you could see that his muscles looked like Popeye.

"Does he dye his hair?"

"Nope, it's black oozing from his devil soul."

"He's scarier than ever."

"We must not waiver from our cause," I said. But she was just talking anyway. Weiggle hadn't figured out how we ever maneuvered in through our secret window. But we had to be quiet as air, I told her. In the window well lay dirty leaves, dead mice, pee, candy wrappers, cigarette butts, stale bread and night crawlers, and sometimes even a dead bird with its feet straight up.

We tightened our lips so we wouldn't holler as we stepped in the mess of the deep window well. I could barely squeak through. Glorybe was bigger-boned than me. But we were both almost five-five. My father measured Annie and me on the dining room closet door and wrote it in ink every year. His writing looked like he'd copied script from the gravestones. I wondered if he believed the measurements would still be there when we were all dead. And I wondered why they didn't put the height people were on the gravestones, to give us a picture of how they looked.

My sneaker stuck on the ledge. I couldn't even yell for Glorybe to help. But Glorybe realized and wedged a stick in and my foot moved just before my strength gave out. I jumped down into the cool Sunday school room. Then she jumped down, with a piece of rotten apple sticking to her sneaker. "No," I said, "don't take the time to clean it."

We tiptoed past the stacked chairs and long tables and shelves with white dishes and white napkins and candlesticks all waiting for a church supper. Past the kitchen and up the back stairs, listening, listening.

"Is the devil as powerful as God?" Glorybe whispered.

"Sometimes the devil wins, that's why we battle him like the dickens."

We ran to the sanctuary door, opened it and rushed into safety. Because the sound of my heart filled my ears I waited until it quieted down. Weiggle hadn't heard us.

We ran down the aisle to the stairs to the balcony. Above the balcony was the trapdoor in the ceiling that led the way on up to the top of the tower. She stepped onto the balcony first. "Can't help it, Indian blood."

We hung over the balcony looking down at the pews to be sure Weiggle wasn't coming back. As I stood there I imagined the congregation in their Sunday hats and wished I was old enough to wear beautiful hats like Annie with two yellow water lilies made of silk. I had just a plain straw hat but Mom put a nice wide blue silk ribbon around it.

Mom wore mostly green to show off her reddish hair. Sometimes she and Easter traded hats when they got tired of their own. Mom said that Easter's hats were flamboyant, which she told me meant like flames. I thought I would like to be full of flames when I grew up.

The bell rope hung from the balcony ceiling, thick as a tiger's tail. It rang automatically except for special occasions, like Sundays or weddings. Dad let me help him ring the bell one Sunday to announce church when Weiggle was on vacation. Dong, dong dong, you could hear it all over town, telling people, "Wake up you lazy bones, come to church, come to church."

Even Dad had to pull with all his might to get the rope started. His eyebrows arched upward to their limits with each pull. And once his glasses fell off. Then the bell, the great, booming, jangling, crushing, banging, deep down iron bell rang out, ruckusing in my chest. "Hang on tight," Dad said. The coarse rope dug at my hands but up it took me up, quick as a gas balloon.

Then the rope rose up and down by itself with me hanging on for dear life. Nothing felt like this. I loved the thrill. I imagined that above, through the ceiling, God was raising me up and suddenly dropping me down. Maybe it was because I would get too close to the mysteries of God or maybe the devil, that Dad wouldn't take me up inside, though he said it was because the tower was too dirty.

"Where are the pigeons?" Glorybe asked.

"The top, I think. There will be plenty so your dad will dance."

The long wooden ladder to get to the trapdoor was lying all along the wall. It took two of us to drag it out. "One, two, three." Up to the trapdoor.

I'd never been that high on a ladder. Besides it was old. I wondered if it would break. When I looked at Glorybe's face I said, "Okay, I'll climb first." But I hoped I could open the trapdoor, it was heavy and cumbersome.

My face started sweating. I counted, sixteen rungs. When I reached the ceiling I called, "Hold the ladder." The door spring wouldn't budge. I pushed and pushed until it cried out one last creak of the hinges and gave up the ghost. I swung the door back and laid it on the floor above me.

I looked up into the tower into night blackness. The only light came through the trapdoor itself. I waited for God to grab me but when He didn't I dared to pull myself up onto the floor and looked back through the hole at Glorybe.

"Quick." If evil or goodness was going to strangle me I wanted her there to save me. I held the top of the ladder and she clutched her sneakers onto each rung. I pulled her inside fast.

We stayed very still, our eyes straining at the darkness and then we saw her. Made me jump at the sight…the bell like a lady with a monster-sized skirt, the great bell. I bent over and peered up under. "Wow, the clapper is the size of a dragon's tongue." I ran my hands along it, bumpy and cool, amazingly heavy.

"How did they get the bell through the trapdoor?" Glorybe asked.

"Maybe they built the church around it."

"So they'll have to tear the church down if she gets a crack like the Liberty Bell?"

"Church bells don't get cracks. They're already holy."

She gave me a punch. "It's a good thing it isn't ringing now," she said.

"Yeah, one ring would split our head wide open."

"And make us deaf."

The smell resembled dead frogs or burning leaves or rotten onions, old wasp nests and bat dung, mice turds and squirrel, a smell like you shouldn't be there, like death roamed inside. I wondered again if Dad didn't want me there because of something more than just dust and creaky stairs, something strange, something that could take me away from him.

We tiptoed around the great bell, trying to find how to climb to the next level. "We've got to do it fast in case Weiggle sees the ladder and the bell will ring in an hour," I warned.

"Why doesn't anybody dust this place? What's that over there?" "Bats," I said. "They like tangling in blond hair."

"Get me out of here."

"Don't worry they sleep all day. That's why they're called bats, they're batty."

We could just about make out the stairs. But we had a lot higher to go, two more levels, to where the pigeons must be nesting. Glorybe volunteered to go first. Another trapdoor but that one she just slid off. It had no spring. The light struck us from everywhere. "The round window room. From hell into heaven," I said. "Only one more level to go." We hugged and jumped up and down. But dust filled our throats so we stopped.

The round window room. Windows all the way around. You could see the top of our sycamore tree and see Jeremiah mowing our lawn. You could see Ansier's broken chimney, the candy store, the cemetery and the park and Jeremiah's house tucked in tight with the others. Even a sliver of the river flashed here and there like a scarf in the breeze.

I said, "Throw thyself down and the angels will bear thee up..." quoting the devil's temptation to Jesus.

"Stop it," Glorybe said, "you're giving me the creeps."

But I thought I was even more scared than she. I almost felt I might jump. But Glorybe pulled me away. We kept on moving. When I put my foot on the last ladder I couldn't believe what a rickety piece of junk it was. She said, "I'll hold it for you."

"Plenty of feathers," I reassured her. "Do you hear them flapping around above us? What if they're really angels? White feathers with golden tips. The Indian would give us the dance of our lives wouldn't he? He would fly with the feathers."

I climbed slowly, the ladder waved back and forth like sheets on a line. I counted out loud to keep up my courage, twenty rungs. At the top I called, "I bet this ladder was made when the church was built in seventeen something."

"Stop it." Now she wasn't kidding.

I didn't talk. I almost didn't dare. I had to pretend to her the rungs were strong. "It's fine." But she knew the ladder was fluttering, she was holding onto it. I didn't look down. I was touching the last trapdoor. But I stood under it afraid I'd lose my balance on that ghastly ladder. I didn't dare move to slide the trapdoor. "What are you doing?" Glorybe asked.

"Don't talk."

I reached up, pushed it over and pulled myself up very carefully. I could feel the ladder shudder as I eased myself up.

"They're thousands," I said. "Come on up."

"No."

"You got to see them."

"No. I'm not coming."

"Yes, you are."

"You can't tell me what to do."

"Glorybeee..."

"You get the feathers yourself. It doesn't take two of us."

"If you don't come we're through forever and I mean it."

She thought about that. "I don't care."

"Did you know this from the beginning? You just got me up here knowing you never intended to go all the way? Yellow belly."

"You're the one who's yellow," she yelled. "You went first so I'd hold the ladder."

"I'll hold it for you from here."

"No deal."

"Glorybe, then this is it. We're finished."

"I'm leaving," she said and she let go of the ladder. I took a deep breath and took the chance that she wouldn't desert me and I entered the room of the pigeons. That was the highest place I'd ever been. The room was the smallest and had no windows, just slats open to the air and it was full of pigeons flipping in and out. I stepped to the middle and they grew frantic.

So this was the seat of God's spirit. This must be the innermost sacred place. This was what the choir sang to. This was what Dad meant when he said, "Lift up your hearts."

The small circular room teemed with birds that were growing more agitated as I stepped in their way, raising my hands to try and grab them for some feathers. They dove from their roosts and swooped around me.

A wing grazed my lips. I shut my eyes and I stood stark still. Feathers stroked my face and hair. They flew faster, dipping and diving. As I turned around more and more rose up like flying ribbons on Maypoles, swinging in toward me and swinging outward. They brushed against me in shocking warmth. I twirled round to excite them so they'd rush at me more. They hurt, yet they felt smooth and wonderful, like the shock of the cold river on a hot day. I let my head fall back and they brushed my throat and arms. Fluttering and fanning. I shut my eyes.

"Are you coming or not?" Glorybe called. "Hurry up. I want to get out of here. The bell might ring."

I tore off my shirt. I couldn't move. I raised my arms up high. I swayed back and forth. The birds flew under my hair. Swept across my naked breasts, my arms and back, but my bare bud breasts wanted them the most. I was in a wheezing trance.

"Theodora," she yelled.

I couldn't answer. I was dancing around them, turning and spinning. I wanted to keep their wings moving like millions of fingers tips as if giving loving sensations to every part of my body.

"If you don't come I'm leaving."

I heard her start to go but I couldn't leave. The wings never stopped grazing and teasing me with their wild and stinging softness. Was this what Dad never wanted me to know? This strange thrill in the church tower, my awakening to sexual feelings?

"Theodora!!!"

"Okay," I said, weak-like. I pulled my shirt back on. I scooped up a handful of feathers. I looked back at the angel-birds. I paused. "I'll be back," I promised them.

I stared down the hole. "Glorybe, hold the ladder."

She came back and held the ladder. "Hurry up, the bell is going to ring soon." So in the middle of my climb she let go. I skidded down fast, the ladder almost flipping over, and I yelped as

I touched the floor. But Glorybe was not there. She had skittered down the next and then the next ladder.

At the last trapdoor she stopped dead. When I got there I saw why. There was no ladder, nothing was there. Nothing between us and the balcony floor far below. "Weiggle," I said.

"What do we do?"

"Yellow bellies never know what to do." I took a quick look at her face, bright as the stove burner. She was hopping mad too.

I called out, "Help." But the church was empty.

We both hollered, very loud, "Help, help." I was dying for a drink after the scorching heat of the tower. "Help, help, oh please help us."

The bell might ring. Left here to die or go deaf. Four days until Sunday. Who would know we were here? And Mom and Dad wouldn't think to look in the tower and Weiggle probably wanted us to die.

My head hurt from leaning down through the hole, the dust from the floor was clogging my nose. But I wasn't going to cry. Not on your life.

Glorybe was lying down on the other side of the trapdoor. She stopped calling too. My Dad couldn't hear me. Mrs. Shrimp, Dad's secretary, couldn't. Or Mom or Suzy or Annie with her sharp ears or anybody outside.

The bell rope that came through the ceiling was too far out of our reach to grab and swing down onto the balcony and we were higher up than my bedroom window.

"Why don't you say a prayer?" Glorybe asked. She meant it. Then she said, "Never mind, I'll say one, what do I say?"

"Dear God in heaven, get us the heck out of here."

She said it out loud. Then the door opened by the pulpit and Weiggle walked in. "Beginner's luck," I said to her.

"Mr. Weiggle," I called politely, "Could you please put the ladder back?" He looked around, like pretending he didn't know where we were.

"Mr. Weiggle, up here."

He looked up from way up front by the pulpit. He squinted. He acted innocent. But then he said, "Oh, I knew you was there."

"Let us down, please," I said in my Sunday school voice.

"Will he do it, will he?" Glorybe whined.

"Be quiet," I said. "Please, Mr. Weiggle." He limped his polio leg to the back of the church and sat down.

"Mr. Weiggle, please."

He got up. "I think you have a lesson to learn, so no. No." He walked toward the door. He went out and shut it.

"What are we going to do?" Glorybe was crying. "I wished we'd never crossed him."

"I think we should scream."

We screamed, which did no good.

We lay on the floor with our faces hanging over the edge. We knew we couldn't jump. "I'm so thirsty," she said.

"Me too."

"We're going to die, aren't we?" she hollered. "You and your ideas."

Then we saw the door open again. We heard him. He climbed the side steps, slide, bump slide, bump, like a hideous criminal. He appeared on the balcony, underneath us and looked up stiffly as if he had a sore neck.

"Your explanation about what you're doing there better be good." He folded his arms over his chest. He looked very very old in his silly leather shorts.

"You took the ladder away," I said.

"We went to get some pigeon feathers," Glorybe explained, to cheer up my father to dance. He's very sick."

Was she lying? I didn't know he was *very* sick. But I couldn't think about that now. I dug out the feathers from my shorts' pocket and showed him.

"You aren't allowed up there." He didn't budge toward the ladder, lying against the wall.

"I didn't know," I said contritely. For a second I thought about the wonderful pigeon wings, guiltily, like he would know what I'd been up to. "We won't do it again. We both promise." Then I whispered to Glorybe, "Stop crying. He'll be so happy if he sees your tears."

"You promise, Theodora?"

Very softly I said, "Yes," while crossing my fingers.

"And you'll never come in the church and play and mess up again and bother the living daylights out of me?"

I swallowed. "I promise." I kept my fingers crossed.

"You'll do your messing in the park or the river or in your own back yard? Even if you don't mess, no playing in my clean church."

"I promise." I crossed my fingers on my other hand.

"Swear on the Bible? I've got lots of troubles of my own with my teenage kids. I don't need you brats. And I'm going to tell your father."

"If you do I'll tell about how your dogs poop all over and sometimes you forget for a long time to clean it up."

"Is he going to save us?" Glorybe whispered. I couldn't answer. We heard the scraping as he dragged the ladder. He took his sweet time setting up the ladder. Why was he climbing up himself? Was he going to kill us? Oh God, oh God. But when he was on the last rung he held out a Bible. "Both of yous put your hands on." We did quick as a flash. "Now swear you'll never come in this place again." We both swore. And I quickly crossed my fingers again.

He climbed down and he held the ladder but my heart was throbbing. I didn't trust him, would he let the ladder go and say it was an accident? I tried to figure his face. I never could figure out his nasty look. Glorybe wanted to go first. She made it but that didn't mean he'd let me, his archenemy.

I set my foot on the first rung. He hadn't moved. I put my foot on the second rung. Throb. My heart. Then I scrambled down so fast it almost didn't matter that the rungs were under me. I jumped the last four rungs to the floor.

When we were safe I shouted as I ran, "I don't make promises to Lucifer on the holy Bible."

"And it isn't just your church," Glorybe had the nerve to yell.

I ran. Glorybe ran right behind me.

Weiggle yelled back. "You little scums. If you come in here again there's going to be hell to pay and I mean it."

"Hell," I said to Glorybe, "See he used the word hell, that shows you where he's from."

But I knew he wouldn't tell Dad because of his pooping dogs.

Safe in the yard the bell began to ring the hour, three times. Then I remembered how Glorybe wouldn't climb the ladder and how she stopped holding it for me. I took the feathers out and threw them into the wind.

"There's your feathers. I never want to see you again."

Glorybe didn't move...then she bent to gather the feathers. She walked away from me, slowly, her head high, her hair blowing so you could see her bright pink scalp looking raw as a burn.

CHAPTER 7

$\mathcal{I}$ was awfully conflicted about Glorybe because of The Indian. How long would I hold this position? To distract my ache I wandered out to the hedge to hang around Dad and Jeremiah. Jeremiah wasn't clipping our hedge. He was pacing up and down with Dad. Because of their intensity I sneaked close to listen.

"Mrs. Strickland was acting real snippy with me. Then she came right out.

She told me she didn't want any nigger and 'particularly you, you big black nigger,' around in her yard any more. 'I don't trust you.'"

"How terrible," Dad said. He spotted me. "How about getting us some sassafras, Sweetpea?"

I started to move slowly away but still listening.

Dad said to Jeremiah, "That's horrible what she said to you. So sorry, Jeremiah." He touched his shoulder. "Do you need some money?"

He shook his head no. He had his pride. But I knew their dinners were slim.

"I didn't tell her I was home when her husband was murdered. She wanted to believe what she wanted."

I kept walking at a snails pace.

I called back hoping to make Jeremiah feel better. "Will you play checkers with me."

They didn't talk more until I was out of reach.

I kept imagining Strickland's big belly again sogged, ripped up, decaying like a rotted pumpkin and near where we played.

We were hunched over the checker board and that's when I asked, "Jeremiah, please tell me down-south stories."

"So you're walking under a cottonwood tree." He looked up at our sycamore tree we were sitting under. "Just imagine the juicy black snakes draped like Christmas chains all over the branches. Watch yourself, one of them is bound to leap around your neck like a stunning necklace." He laughed.

I screamed and jumped. "I was glad to leave there for other reasons, though."

"Like what?" I crowned a checker. I grinned at Jeremiah in triumph. But he kept that confident look. No cleft appeared in his chin, like when he's anxious.

"You and I could never be friends. Down there if I even passed by a white girl I was supposed to drop my eyes straight to the ground." He screwed his face up.

"You mean you couldn't even speak to her?"

"Absolutely not. Not, if the girl didn't speak first."

"But what if you spoke first?"

"Oh there'd be hell to pay. Probably a bunch of white folks would come do me some kind of damage. It's so different here."

"What kind of damage?" I stopped playing.

"Beat me up, steal from me, and scare me badly. Just plain folks, maybe somebody you know and you couldn't imagine what's in their hearts. That's why my sister and I decided to be white folks."

"White folks? What do you mean?"

"When I was in first grade we mixed up whitewash, like you put on fences, and slathered it over our faces and arms and let it dry and then sneaked to school that way. In the south Whites went to White schools and Colored to Colored schools. We walked into our classroom, real happy but our teacher Miss Hall grabbed us at the door.

She asked us what we thought we were doing coming to school looking like ghosts. We told her we were going to be White from then on. She looked stunned and sent us home and told us to come back after we washed up. All the kids laughed and teased us for weeks after. But the north is different as different can be. That's why I'm here. And the river's got no snakes."

"I'm so glad you live in the north and in our town and near me. Those people sound awful. What a mean bunch of kids, laughing. It isn't fair, Jeremiah, I can lie out in the sun and get dark as a plum, but you can't get a whit lighter, no matter what."

"Maybe if I was to soak in Clorox." He chuckled.

"You're not winning this game," I said, but he did.

CHAPTER 8

$\mathcal{I}$ stood in front of Glorybe's house, getting up the nerve to call for her. Now, I finally said to myself and I climbed onto the porch. The door was shut. My knock was weak. When I knocked louder Glorybe's mother answered, looking like a scarecrow, her hair up in blue curlers. She had on a worn white bathrobe and her sourpuss face.

"What do you want?"

"Glorybe," I said in a whisper.

"She's asleep. You can't just come over here at eight-thirty in the morning. My husband is asleep too. He's not so well. I've got to go look for work. I've got to start making money. If he's out too long he might be fired and you wouldn't know what that was like, now would you? You got a house and food and I heard the church pays for the gas in your father's car and the heat in your house. You wouldn't know what it is to be hungry, would you?" She was talking fast.

"We were migrants. We were pickers, my mom and dad and six brothers, and you couldn't leave that work your whole life once you got into it. You didn't have money to leave. No car, no trolleys or buses near by. Sometimes people left a baby to die beside the road because they couldn't feed another mouth. Some people ran off and nobody ever heard of them again. They probably starved to death. And it don't feel good to starve. Your belly swells up with air and you want to burst with pain..."

I held my stomach. "How did you get here?" I asked, amazed that she would tell me her life when she had hardly ever talked to me before. She went on, almost as if she didn't know I was there. "I met The Indian in our town. He was driving through North Carolina to see his sister, who had T.B. and he was having coffee in the shop. We never went to town but my mom made me go to a real doctor in town, who took us free, for this infected toe I had from banging into some machinery. The doctor cut my sore and let the puss run out and it was god-dammed sore and I was hobbling to go the five miles back to the fields when he comes up to me, this big tall agile man."

Her face lit up like I'd never seen before.

"I loved the sight of him and he opened his car door for me and he took me in his car and I never went back. Never looked back, neither. Just ran off from my old man and lady and those endless fields. I wrote them a postcard but I never went back. And you can bet your bottom dollar my brothers still got deep cuts on their fingers from the cotton they'll go on plucking until they keel over in the swelter."

"Wow," I said. That was the first time I thought of her as a person. Then I saw Glorybe had come to stand behind her mother, peeking out.

"Glorybe," I said. "Will you play with me?"

"Nope."

I peered to see if The Indian was around. I got a new idea. Annie's going to be out."

"I don't like your ideas anymore. I'm not going with you."

"Come on." My shoulders sank.

"Nope." We looked at each other.

"I want to make up."

"You called me yellow."

"I was just talking about your hair."

"Liar." But I could see she almost smiled.

"You'll miss out."

"I'm not coming." She started to shut the door.

"Okay, okay. I'm sorry."

"How sorry?"

"I'll never call you names again."

She moved away from the door a minute. She came back. "Swear on this and no crossing your fingers," she said. She held out her father's silver bracelet.

She knew I'd never go back on my word now. She must have known how I felt about The Indian and I wondered when he'd dance. For a fleeting moment I wondered if he could charge money to see him dance, if he lost his job, if they needed food.

CHAPTER 9

$\mathcal{G}$lorybe was crying. Her face was all red, "My mom hit my dad with the stew pan. I heard them banging around the kitchen so I ran down stairs. She just picked up the stew pan and whacko she hit him and now he's getting over his shiner. He just sits in his hammock on the porch because he still can't work. He doesn't feel good and now doesn't sleep from his coughing."

I had wished when I was younger that my mom and dad would be exciting like hers. The undertaker, Gruber, asked me when I was about six years old, "How's your mom and dad?"

"They fight like all get-out and really loud," I lied.

"Well, I'll be." His eyes had rolled. "I never heard them."

"They run around the house, breaking things."

"Breaking things? I'll be." He puckered his Cupid mouth. "Like what?"

"Like a big big mirror."

"You mean smashed it? Somebody got hurt?"

I suddenly realized I was in deep water. "I got to go," I said.

But that wasn't the end. Gruber told everybody in our neighborhood and Mom and Dad heard and Dad washed my mouth out with soap. Oh how he hated lying. But mostly when I did something he disapproved of he would give me a look of grave disappointment and I would swear to myself I would never do that again, at least for that day. And Mom dragged me to Gruber and made me tell him that my story was just a story. Gruber promised he would straighten out all the neighbors.

"Let's cheer up your dad, when he wakes up. Maybe if he dances he'll feel better. You still have the feathers don't you?"

Just then he came out to the hammock. His shiner looked like a patch over his left eye. His long nose and long face seemed to have sunk a bit. I had never seen him like that, slumped and sad. I felt my eyes welling up.

"We got you all the feathers," I said.

"They're on top of the radio," Glorybe said.

He looked up. His eyes focused. He gave me a nod.

"Will you dance for us?" I asked, my face growing bright. He said nothing. He just looked at me a long time, making my heart roar.

He stepped inside. We heard him coughing.

"Will he come back?"

Glorybe shrugged.

We waited. Glorybe's brother came out. He didn't speak to us and we didn't speak to him. He was going to look for a job. The WPA wouldn't take him. He was too young.

The Indian did come back. On his head was a headdress of our twelve feathers pushed into the holes of a belt and the belt was buckled around his head.

I'd never seen the braid, the whole thing. He always doubled it over but now he let it free and it looked like a long beautifully braided rope. On his feet were moccasins crowded with beads. He was wearing blue jeans and an open leather vest. His tan hairless chest was curved like a shield and the color of the chamois cloth that Dad used to polish our car.

He was wearing more jewelry than I had ever seen, bracelets and rings and two silver necklaces with green and aqua stones. He was glorious beyond what I dreamed.

Songs came from down deep in his throat. His voice rose and fell, sad and fetching as some night bird. As he moved his feet slowly over the porch he waved his arms like swallows dipping... like the birds in the tower softly stroking me. It was as if he were stroking me. His palms faced toward me. He bent his knees low and kicked his feet one at a time, carefully so you could see how he did it. Padding, padding on the old boards. His face was turned toward the sky and he moved around so we could see all of his supple body, as his arms fluttered faster and faster, as if they were whirling toward me. He was singing sensuous words I couldn't understand. I didn't want to take my eyes from him, ever, dreaming he was my destiny, which in a way came true.

CHAPTER 10

The Depression had slowly come to my consciousness and disturbed my secure world as I began to realize that Glorybe and Jeremiah's families could be going hungry. I wished Glorybe and I could make money and then an idea presented itself as Dad called, "Come here, inside the garage." A big mystery was plastered all over his face.

"Something I promised you for ages. Your birthday present. Happy thirteen."

"For ages." I was jumping up and down. I didn't want to hope. Dad had moved the car out and in the middle was a huge box with the words, Cris-craft. He helped me open it, tearing and cutting. Glorybe and I hugged. Annie and Suzy and Mom were all waiting but they knew what was inside. I jumped like I was ready to jump right over the trees. And Glorybe held me around the waist, jumping too.

"A kayak to build," I screeched.

I had dreamed of this moment my entire life, my own kayak, flat bottomed slithering over rocks, me on the river, free on the river.

Dad laid out the pieces to assemble. He took Glorybe and me outside to the rain barrel. "Soak the wood and when it is soft enough to bend we form the ribs."

Before us began to appear a skeleton, long and skinny as a trout. "Now comes the skin," Dad said.

We stretched the canvas as tight as we could. I told The Indian later.

"Did you ever have a boat?" I asked him.

"No, I don't think so."

Jeremiah stopped mowing the lawn and came in. "I never had a boat, but Erasmus Dugan and I made a raft and I stole a rope from Mrs. Longman's clothesline for tying the logs. But me and Erasmus fell out and the raft got washed away forever and my pappy said, 'God locks his fingers on wrong doings and he doesn't give you the pleasure of having pleasure.'"

"It was only a clothesline rope. Do you believe your pappy?"

He patted the bow of my boat. His face screwed up and made that familiar cleft in his chin deeper. "Most of the time."

"What do you mean?"

"Sometimes people do wrong and get pleasure doing wrong. But you don't want to meet those people on a dark moonless night in the middle of a rainy forest."

Then he helped us seal all the seams with goop. But kind of messy like the way he cuts the hedge, lumps and valleys, though I have to admit I wasn't any better. I clasped my hands in admiration. My very own boat.

Maybe I would never want anything more in my whole life. A thrill started in my belly and went down somewhere secret below.

"Thank you, Dad. Thank you Glorybe, Thank you for helping, Jeremiah."

Glorybe and I took the kayak out in the driveway and painted it a heavenly blue. Nobody else I knew had a boat.

"What name should we call it?" I asked.

"White Horse, after my granddaddy," Glorybe said.

"But it's blue."

"I know."

"Let's call it the Ark after Noah's Ark."

She chewed her lip. She flipped her hair. She stood on one foot and hopped around, thinking.

I called inside to Dad. "What do you think?"

"How about the Titanic?"

"Oh Daddy," I screeched.

The next few days, Glorybe had me worried about The Indian. Five days he had been away from work and after ten days they would fire him. He just couldn't go to work yet, he kept saying, while he was still coughing.

I was frantic. That's when I got the idea, "We can sell tickets for rides on the river and give money to The Indian, maybe some to the Johnsons."

"It's never going to rain enough for your boat to get a good ride in that river, way too shallow and rocky until you get to Perth Amboy," she said.

"Come on," I said. "We just need a good rain."

Suzy overheard. "Only if you clean the junk from under your bed."

"Then what?"

"Then it will rain."

I didn't believe her but just in case I moved the junk from under my bed to the closet. Yet still it didn't rain. I was tearing my hair. I was splitting a gut, as Annie liked to say. Waiting, waiting, waiting.

I hung around Dad and Jeremiah. They were in the backyard digging up fishing worms.

Jeremiah said, "I got questioned today. Nothing much from that silly detective, Leonardo, asking if I liked Strickland and why did the Mrs. fire me? And I just said that I didn't dislike Mr. Strickland and that I didn't really know why she fired me. Probably just hitting out, from her mourning. I didn't tell the awful names Mrs. Strickland had called me."

"What did that Leonardo say to that?" Dad asked.

"He said, 'I bet.' Asked me if I liked to fish and when I said everybody around here likes to fish. He said he don't. Only Coloreds like to fish. Then he said, as he left, 'we're not finished.'"

Dad said, "Don't worry. He doesn't have a leg to stand on."

"I'm not really worried," Jeremiah answered. They moved slowly away. Jeremiah went through the hedge to sweep the sidewalk.

CHAPTER 11

*T*hree days later the clouds were darkening and grew thick as Suzy's molasses pudding. I ran across the street to Glorybe's. "It's raining," I hollered.

We ran and got Bess-the-Mess to come. She was rich and she had a friend who after this trip we never saw again. I can't remember her name. We charged them 25 cents apiece to give to Glorybe's family and Jeremiah's. That was a lot of money then. It would buy milk and bread and eggs.

The rain came in torrents, a hullabaloo dinning away on our roof. Now the river would be swollen enough but I had no real concept of how fierce it had become. Dad wasn't home, thank goodness. For certain he wouldn't have allowed us to go and years later he confessed that was the worst moment in his life.

I ran to Mom. "Okay, you can go but only as far as Peter's Bend," she said. She didn't know too much about rivers and she couldn't imagine what ours looked like then. Glorybe wouldn't think of telling her mother or The Indian.

I really didn't have any idea of the fierceness either, although an inkling came to mind. Bess-the-Mess came with a friend. We didn't call Bess that to her face. My sister liked to say she wasn't the sharpest pencil in the box. But we liked her because she knew a lot of stuff about boys and told us all sorts of lies about the sex act, which we believed.

The downpour was a dense curtain now but I was choking on my willpower. The shortcut through the woods contained many thick vines, which had brought down some of the trees. We passed the tree that Glorybe and I had carved with our initials and the date. The four of us slithered The Ark through. The rain flew at our faces and through our shorts and shirts, plastering them to our skin. The shortcut took us longer than the road. And I kept saying, "Don't scratch Noah's Ark's bottom."

Then we giggled our heads off. Bess-the-Mess didn't know whether to laugh or cry and the other girl looked nervous. But we had their 50 cents.

I couldn't believe the river, an erupting, churning mass of white, white foam. You felt like the river was going to flood the banks, flood your insides. The water grew as noisy as a hammering, racing train, splashing us hard as we gaped at the sight.

"Maybe we shouldn't go," Glorybe said.

The friend of the Mess just stared, pinching her teeth against her lip. Bess-the-Mess was wearing a halter-top and very tight shorts. She shaved her legs. Our mothers wouldn't let us...or cake on any lipstick. The name of which The Mess said was plum sensation. She also went to school in her mom's heels. Her mom owned a hairdresser shop over in Linden. She did up the Mess's hair. It looked like some kind of a nest full of sticks, with all the bobby pins showing. And it was different colors, sometimes blond, or red with streaks of black. She was practically a grownup, fifteen, but she stayed back in school twice and so was in our grade.

"We can't go," Glorybe said.

"Are you nuts? We waited a lifetime," I said. But I was in the worst doubt. I'd never in my whole life seen the river like this. Even so, I thought we could stop at Peter's Bend. The river slowed down there.

"I'm not sure we can get in," Glorybe said.

"It looks like a milkshake," The Mess said.

We walked along the bank.

"It looks fatal," Glorybe said.

We were near Jeremiah's house hoping Eliah and Selina would help.

"We can't even get in," Glorybe said.

"Yeah," The Mess said.

"Come on. You paid good money. Don't worry, we'll look for a muddy spot next to the river, put the boat down and shove ourselves out with the paddles," I yelled above the roar.

"Think that will work?" The friend said without letting lose her teeth holding her lip so I barely heard.

"No," I whispered to myself. But nothing would stop me. I wanted desperately to help, mostly The Indian.

"Will we be able to stop at Peter's Bend?" Glorybe yelled.

"Of course. Think of Noah. He didn't hesitate."

She rubbed her face to erase her alarm and at that point the Mess's friend left, yelling back, "You can keep my quarter."

We ran to get Eliah and Selina. "You're crazy," Eliah said, chewing his fingernails. But Selina shouted, "Next time is my turn." They both helped us anyway, laying the Ark on a level spot.

"You promise to take me next time," Selina said again.

We climbed in, our paddles ready. The Mess sat in the middle.

"And no wiggling I warned. There was barely room.

"I wouldn't do this," Eliah said. "I mean if you fell out you'd go under so fast you wouldn't even have time to holler."

"I'm getting out," the Mess said.

"We're not falling out. It's flat bottomed for rapids." But she jumped out and said like her friend, "You can keep the quarter." I didn't even answer but I wanted to call her a sissy. I wiggled into position in front, Glorybe in back, and I was glad I couldn't see her frightened face. They pushed us through the mud and into the water and the rapids hit us like a truck emptying coal down a shoot.

The river carried us fast as a roller coaster, up and over rocks and into foam--foam you could almost float on, foam like an enormous bubble bath, but the scariest bubble bath on earth, I thought. No time to breathe or think.

I yelled, "Duck," as we saw a tree uproot and crash smack over the river. We skittered underneath. A small branch, sharp as a glasscutter, scratched my face.

Right then Glorybe yelled, "I lost my paddle." Without her paddle we couldn't stop at Peter's Bend. Yet I knew paddles were of no use, even though I held mine as if it could save my life.

I didn't yet think we were going to die. Not until the river narrowed and I knew I was on a fatal path and I was all alone. Nobody was in the boat. Maybe Glorybe wasn't there anymore, even though she was there. I couldn't think or scream. Anyway the river-roar would have drowned my screams.

That was my first knowledge of how selfish nature was, didn't care about us and nature was not a part of us, but a separate entity that we visited. Mother nature was sometimes benign, caressing, whispering sweetness, sometimes as vicious as a dog crunching a mole…a psychotic mother. We were no more than leaves that had fallen in, and its only job was to carry us downstream in any careless ripping way it felt like.

The river was king. The river was God and death, and God and death was the same thing. My paddle slipped away. I hung onto the sides of the kayak. We spun and spun as the river slapped us over mounds of water, whirling me sick. I wished I could shut my eyes. I wished I could throw up. I didn't know if Glorybe was still there as we entered Dunbar Bend, the narrowest of all. Just past the Wheatena factory and where Strickland had been found and where we slid in the mud. But now the river was eating up the bank.

Nobody was going to save us. Nobody knew we were in trouble. Mommy, Daddy, I cried in my heart, save me, knowing this time they couldn't.

Dunbar Bend was a deep cut in the rocks, a tunnel with a strip of blue sky showing. Tall stony banks were on either side where we careened through, fast as steam. Then, strangely, for a second, the boat stopped dead, caught on a rock on the bank.

"Hang on," I shouted, hoping Glorybe was still alive. I clawed at the rock walls to keep the kayak from going plunk down into the river sideways but there was nothing to hang on to. The walls were wet and slick and the river tore us away but we landed okay back in the water.

Right then where the Linden River met the Rahway River everything doubled, the depth of water, the torrent, the noise, the spume. Even my eyes doubled.

We saw that nobody was standing on the bridge to help us. Then came the high dam. We were going to go over it. No question. I think that was my first scream but I might have been screaming the whole way.

I felt the hover, there on the top, a tiny moment of calm, a tiny leftover spark of me before I was gone. That's when I shut my eyes. I couldn't stand seeing myself die. I prayed, "God, please save me, I'll be good forever." We plunged straight over the dam and down, an arrow into the froth.

I was still inside. The boat raced sideways and I looked around. Glorybe was there but like a statue, as if she had fainted sitting straight up, the rain pouring over her. I had forgotten it was raining.

"Look!" I pointed where the Rahway River grew as wide as a football field, and all of a sudden calm. The water lazed out, washing into velvety brown from digging out the banks. I shouted for being alive and Glorybe shouted for being alive. Maybe we were crying or laughing; at any rate we were hysterical and I wet my already soaking shorts.

Some kid waved at us. Poor White people lived here on the banks. The shoes they wore to school were all lopsided. Mom got really mad when I said that they were dumb.

"Never call them dumb. They don't have your advantages. Never say that again."

We tried to row to shore with our hands. It was slow because of having no paddles. "That was so much fun," I hollered back to Glorybe.

"Yeah."

"Let's do it again." We laughed and laughed. Then she was mad at me and yelled, "This is no joke."

Now that we were safe I thought how close to dying we'd been. I used to think living was like a river that you would never see the end of death was too far away. That day I saw the end of my life. I saw how eternal the river was and how ephemeral I was. I thought of what Jeremiah said, that the river gives and the river takes away. I felt sad and wise, as wise as I would ever be.

We couldn't get in to shore. The kid named Joshua saw us and waved. He was in the class ahead of us. He liked numbers and was serious as all get out. But that was good for us right then. I wanted him to help and he knew how. He ran along the bank with his mother's clothesline tied with a huge stick and threw it until we caught it.

After the three of us raised the kayak up onto the bank we lay down, exhausted. The sun had appeared just in time to dry us. Joshua said he could teach us algebra if we wanted.

I said we could teach him kayaking.

"Sure, how about on New Year's Eve." He rolled his eyes.

We lay there hardly able to move. "We shouldn't have done that," Glorybe said.

But we have 50 cents."

We carried The Ark along the dirt road into town. We were a spectacle, wet and filthy. Then we saw him, pacing back and forth and leaning over the Irving Street Bridge. "Dad, Dad. Here we are."

He didn't move at first. I think he didn't believe I was me. Then he came running toward us, Jeremiah with him. Eliah had told him he was worried about us. I never saw Jeremiah's face like that before, his eyelids down and his face sagging and his shoulders in an old position. Dad looked as if he were about to cry. No, my father's face was worse than crying, like something very sick had come to live in him.

"Lucas Stein said he didn't believe anybody could last in that river."

61

Something weird came over me. I hadn't realized what he would feel if I had died. I just thought what I'd feel if he or Mom died. Now I knew that if I had been killed, that would have killed them also.

"Don't tell Mom," I said. "Or Easter."

"Don't tell my parents, please," Glorybe said.

Dad didn't reply. Then the dead look escaped from his face and he came alive, like a flame out of hell and into scorching anger. I'd never seen him that angry. "Down on your knees."

"Dad, not on the bridge...right in the middle of town."

"You heard me, Theodora." He had a look in his eyes as if they were frozen and would never move again.

"You too, Gloria," he ordered.

"Why?"

"To confess to God."

"I'm Indian. We don't talk to God."

"That's okay, you can talk to the moon and stars then."

"What do I say?" She rubbed her tearing eyes.

I covered up my face. This was the worst thing my father had ever done to me. "Dad, please, Bobby Elwood is coming across the bridge."

"Just let him walk by. We're having a session with the Lord, here."

But then the most awful thing happened, Dad knelt down too, right there with us. How could he? It was bad enough making us kneel down in the middle of town, and Jeremiah with him, all four of us, kneeling on the hard cinder-covered bridge.

"What should I say?" Glorybe whispered.

"You say what you have on your heart, both of you."

"Do it fast," I said to Glorybe when I heard Bobby Elwood yell, "Hey, Theodora, what's you doing on your knees?"

I pretended I didn't hear him. Glorybe said quickly, "I pray to the sun and moon and stars that I'll never do that again."

"Fine," Dad said but I could tell his anger hadn't gone yet, his anger at me. I knew he wouldn't let me up if I didn't say the right words, whatever they were. I quavered something out, "Dear God, punish me."

And Jeremiah said, "Amen."

"You just copy him, Jeremiah?" I choked out, doubly betrayed.

"Now you apologize," Dad said sternly.

"I'm sorry, Jeremiah." But I didn't mean it. Not until I had stood up from this embarrassing position. Then the mean thing I had said to him hung on me like a branch caught in the flood.

I wiped my knees where the bridge made corrugated prints. "We'll have to sell your kayak," Dad said.

"Daddy, please. We worked so hard to build it. Years really, because I wanted it my whole life." I sobbed. Dad turned his face away and I saw him wiping his eyes under his glasses. But Jeremiah patted my shoulder like he sometimes did when I was upset. But I pulled away.

"Dad, please don't sell it," I sobbed out.

He cleared his throat like he did before a sermon and said, "All right, Theodora, but it stays in dry dock until you are old enough to know better."

"Will you tell Mommy?"

"And I won't tell your mother. But you promise you won't sneak in the river again."

"I won't tell Easter, either," Jeremiah said. I knew he had forgiven me.

I stopped crying and thought the one thing then that children wanted most was for parents to trust them. But Glorybe didn't trust me anymore and now she had to lie to her mother and The Indian where she had been. I felt bad about that, but worst of all I had made my father live those dreadful hours thinking I was dead.

I stroked the Ark every day and said to her, "Don't worry we'll do it again someday." I laid her beside the garage, under the chestnut tree, over on her stomach, asleep, waiting for me to wake her. I sure wished it would come soon.

And we never gave the 50 cents to The Indian or Jeremiah because it had fallen out of my pocket.

When I shut my eyes at night I liked to feel the roll and dash of the boat and the thrilling drop over the dam, as long as I wasn't really there.

CHAPTER 12

*Y*ears later Mom told me why she believed in action, why she was out to fight for justice for Colored people, because of what happened to her as a young girl.

The morning was dank and misty when my nine-year-old mother and her twelve-year-old sister, Florence, were walking down a dirt shortcut to their school in Kentucky. Jabbering and jostling at each other had kept them from seeing at first. First my mother saw the hat lying in their path.

Through the mist my mother saw something else and whispered, "Look what's that up there?"

"Shoes are dangling from that branch," Aunt Florence answered.

When they looked higher they saw legs attached to the shoes.

Their eyes then made out a figure, a man hanging. But they could not at first believe it. It was John Mason hanging...their family servant as long as the two young girls had been alive.

My mother, holding his crumpled black hat, reached up toward him as though to hand it back and her sister called out, "John Mason, John Mason," not knowing really, not believing, having had the terrible reality of lynching always kept far from them...

The thought hit them, the notion that he might be dead. Screaming in hysteria my mother ran holding the hat against her chest, Florence right behind her and into their house. For a moment my grandfather couldn't understand through their screams. "You stay here," he commanded but they disobeyed and ran behind him praying their father would save John Mason and that he was still alive.

My grandfather scrambled up the oak tree as if he too hoped John Mason were alive but when he cut him down, holding his lifeless body, he felt the chill of him and wailed with his children. Grandfather, not returning on the short cut but walked through their town so the people could see. He called out to the houses, "Shame. Shame."

All day my grandfather and grandmother and my mother and her sister stayed with John Mason's family, rocking with them in grief. That moment of the realization of prejudice tore at my mother, festered into an abscess that would not heal until she acted.

My mother asked my grandfather why they had hanged him and he answered, "There is never a reason."

After that my mother vowed she would do everything she could to help Colored people. At first she thought things might be different in the north, but discovered prejudice lay just beneath the surface.

The second week in August Mom was on the warpath again. One evening at around seven she dressed up and said I could come along with Glorybe. Mom was headed down to the town council with the same group of women that had been with her to the YMCA. She was confident. She was on fire. Easter was walking right beside her, all gung-ho too, not worried then about any consequences.

Easter had her best straw hat sitting tight on her head, giving her a look of quiet dignity. Dad didn't know about the protest, he was conducting a prayer meeting. And actually Mom didn't want him to know. Jeremiah didn't know either; he was at his own prayer meeting. Annie was at the movies. And Suzy liked whatever Mom did.

The way Mom walked was dead serious but it was really funny too, going so fast that she swayed like a windup toy. I wondered if people thought she was drunk. Imagining her drunk was spine tingling. The last minute she added some more Colored people Mrs. Reynolds, Mrs. Smart and Mrs. Carter. All dressed as if going to a funeral.

Glorybe and I marched behind, about a half a block. Mom was shorter than any of them, her feet tinier than anybody's. She bought her Mary James in the children's department with me, which embarrassed me and she wore them even to church, along with me.

We went past Strickland's house and Ansier's the butcher. We passed the cousins' house, but they were inside. We passed the shoemaker, past the firehouse where the men were leaning over their checkerboards, smoking. "Cigarettes are the only fires they put out," I said to Glorybe.

I knew what Dad thought; nothing gets done if your heart isn't in it. Change that and you change the world. But Mom had other plans, other ways to change the world. The women marched through the double doors where the council meeting had begun with all the town council sitting at a table up on a platform. All eight men watched us. Each had an expression as if they'd bitten lemon rind. Mom's reputation preceded her.

Right up front Mom charged the way she does in church and the rest of us followed. Hector Wolff, he was the chairman, looked at me as if…who let you in? I crossed my arms over my chest just like Mom, and Glorybe and I sat right in back of Mom and the others.

Hector Wolff had a gray face. Above that was his bald head, a washed boulder, that you just knew not even a hammer could crack. He had been the superintendent of our Sunday School last year and had this dumb idea of making the boys sit on one side for worship period, and the girls on the other. And like now, he had an icky habit of clearing his throat, but I realized the stuff down there didn't move.

Mom had timed it just right. They were at the point where anybody could speak up about their grievances. She stood as tall as she could but looked vulnerable as well as powerful.

She talked slowly. "I would like, please, to know why Haydock Street has not been paved after the death of Dunbar Jones."

"I'm sorry I don't remember what happened there?" Hector said.

"I wrote you," Mom said."

"I get a lot of letters."

Margaret Dean, Mom's white friend, stood up. "The reason Dunbar died was because of the road."

"Really?" One of the councilmen asked in disbelief.

Margaret Dean went on as calm as a statue. "That road as you know is unsafe with the deep ruts that are never fixed. When Dunbar rode on his bike through the ruts he skidded and his head hit a tree."

"Why was he riding his bike on that road?" Another man asked.

"He lived there. Every child has a right to ride a bike and there are no sidewalks there like there are in the white part of town and if he went to the white part, white kids would jeer him or likely beat him up," Mom said.

Mrs. Smart asked politely, "Have you ever gone down Haydock Street and Lumbard Street when it rains, Mr. Chairman?"

"No," said Hector. "I don't go down Haydock Street and Lombard's a dead end."

The audience snickered.

"It gets so muddy we have trouble keeping our kids clean, or dry. And the mud stains," Easter said, her voice low but determined.

"Maybe they shouldn't play in the street," Hector Wolff said.

Mom stood up again. "I believe you know that there are no backyards."

Margaret Dean spoke up," Why hasn't the town addressed this, particularly after what happened to Dunbar?"

"Are you accusing the council of Dunbar's death?" A big fat councilman boomed out.

"The point is, he's no longer with us," Mom said.

"But you people ought to be used to streets like that where you come from," Hector Wolff said, his mouth hardly moving, like talking to himself.

"We come from Rahway, born and brought up," Mrs. Smart said.

"We simply want to know when it will be paved?" Mom asked.

"Let me see," Hector Wolff said. He shuffled the papers in front of him. "I'm sorry to say, I don't see pavement on the agenda this summer."

The other councilmen nodded.

"Of course not, but we are here to request it be put on the agenda," Mom said.

Another councilman called out, "We could consider it next year."

The budget is full for this year." Hector Wolff cocked his head to the side and the other members nodded, yes.

Mom was barely holding her anger. "We want an answer. A time."

"Can't do that. We'll have to see."

"That is not good enough. You always have money for emergencies. We want to know exactly when," Mom insisted.

Mrs. Hunt, who had said nothing before, tightened her mouth and said, "My Dahlia went to school with muddy wet feet and the teacher wouldn't let her take her shoes off and when she sneaked them off the teacher discovered and made her go to detention all morning."

"Buy boots," somebody in the audience shouted.

I felt bad. They had no money for boots.

"Well," one of the councilmen said, "You know, Ma'am, we--we're not a rich town and you people don't contribute to the revenue."

Mom's face grew bright red and she no longer contained her anger. I felt excited and leery. "Are you telling me that this town is just for the rich, not for all the people?"

"Yes, for people, that is," the same man in the audience called out.

Snickers rose all around the room. But Hector Wolff hit the gavel.

He said, "That's enough," to the man. Then turning to Mom's group said, "We will just have to see. I will tell you that it doesn't seem likely in the near future." He looked at his watch. "It's getting late I think this discussion is over." He hit the gavel. "Meeting adjourned. All in favor say aye."

The audience rose to leave. As the councilmen came off the podium Mom yelled, "These citizens elected you to take care of them properly." Mom hit her fist on the top of the bench in front of her and shook her hand where it hurt and then followed Hector Wolff out the door, rushing ahead of her friends. That's when I think I really drew a breath and ran after her with Glorybe.

When my feet reached the sidewalk there she was charging up to Hector Wolff, her mouth drawn as if she had a toothache.

"How can you act so insensitively, Hector? You a member of our church, shame on you."

"Pardon me, Mrs. Davis, I think you're trying to have undue influence and this board doesn't take to that. This is a democracy."

"How dare you call what you are doing anything close to democracy?"

"How dare you question these elected officials. Look, you're beating the wrong drum." He paused to think something over. "Look here, I want to warn you, it's a thankless and harmful game you're playing here," he said more softly, almost kindly, like a father to a stupid child. "They don't really care. They are used to living the way they always lived. White folks getting in there is what makes them dissatisfied. I'd stay out of it. It isn't healthy for them." He paused a moment. "And I might say you're even inciting trouble. Yes, with Jeremiah Johnson's name being brought up for working for Mr. Strickland when he was murdered." He shook a finger at Mom. "You might be inciting to riot and that's against the law."

Mom moved in close to him. Her hat had slipped to one side. She was shaking with fury. And almost as if she were about to kiss him, like the movies, she stood on her tiptoes. But instead of kissing him she opened the palm of her right hand, raising it up, short Mom, and with one fell swoop slapped him right across his cheek, as hard as she could.

He spun backward. "I wouldn't have done that if I were you. It certainly is not going to help your cause or Colored people. Everyone is going to hear about this one." He walked quickly past her, rubbing his face.

Mom marched away as her friends rushed to be with her, talking in amazement and awe. I wished I had a false face.

When we reached our door I asked, "Are you going to tell Dad what you did?"

"I'm thinking it over," she said. But Dad was still not home.

The next night Mom was snuggled on Dad's lap in his big reading chair, looking as small as a teddy bear. When she had to tell him something and she didn't want to, she stared into his eyes. And he knew. He was waiting. I could see his face, like he had a mouth full of candy that was too sweet. "At the council meeting last night..."

"Yes?"

"Not good."

Pause.

"How do you mean?"

Pause.

"They aren't going to pave the Colored sections. And I got really mad."

"And did you show it?" He sat up straight.

"Yes, I did."

"Elisabeth, what did you say?"

"It wasn't what I said."

She slid off his lap and faced him. She looked so fragile. He looked so strong. She couldn't seem to figure out how to say what happened. He was waiting. The look on his face was like the candy had gone sour.

"Chester," she said, "It isn't what I said."

"What do you mean?"

"It's what Hector said. He won't even consider paving the Colored street and he had the nerve to say I was stirring up trouble, inciting to riot and even mentioned Jeremiah as if he was a suspect in murder, of all things. I got so mad that I..."

"What?"

"I slapped him right in the face."

"You didn't, you're kidding, of course." He started to chuckle.

"Yes I did."

"Theodora?" he asked me.

"She did." I said, biting my lip.

"Elisabeth, but you apologized profusely?"

"I didn't apologize."

"You didn't? You didn't?"

"No. He should apologize to all the Colored people in this town. I did the right thing to that man."

Daddy got to his feet. He paced the floor and came back. "You must apologize."

"I will not."

"How would it be if I went around slapping people in our congregation because I think they're wrong? He's a member of our church. But that doesn't even matter, even if he weren't."

"No, he should apologize to the Colored people."

Now Daddy pinched his eyes, set his jaw. "You did this in front of Theodora. We don't believe in that kind of behavior to get what we want. How could you go dashing in with no thought? And hitting?"

"Slapping," Mom corrected.

"But you can't believe injury is the way to justice."

"You're right, I don't, but under certain circumstances we have to act, like war to bring peace." Mom stormed out of the room, past me.

"Elisabeth..." he rushed after her. A door slammed somewhere in the house. He came back.

"You want to know why Colored people should be laying low? People have strong feelings and when you mess around with tradition, even bad traditions, people get really stubborn and mean as wasps. Things get worse not better. It can't be sudden process, changing people for the good takes time and words and often the spirit of God, not violence."

Now I climbed on Dad's lap as if a boogie man were after me, as if I were five years old and I smelled the soap lather from his shaving, the odor of spicy sand, and I was thoroughly under his spell. But I knew right then that I inherited something even stronger from Mom.

CHAPTER 13

$\mathcal{I}$ realized lots of people were going hungry, jumping freight trains to find a better place, hitch hiking to the next town, and then the next, hoping. Every day men came to our door to beg for a meal. But most terrible of all, The Indian was fired.

That morning when I called for Glorybe he was lying inside on the couch. He looked so wan and thin that I almost cried. But he said, "Theodora, minister's kid, what badness are you up to?"

"Badness?"

What we were about to do was secret because the grownups might try and stop us. I swallowed hard and didn't answer.

There was still an innocent fervor about us, unharmed by TV or violent movies that in later decades would erode childhood. We were children, yet with new desires of which we hardly were aware, stirrings that were becoming more attuned to our bodies and less to our brains. But fervor for other things we still had.

We hadn't reached the lazy, lie around and primp stage yet, like Annie. We were going to save The Indian.

We dressed in our Sunday best and marched down Union Street and Church Street. On our heads were our Easter hats all except The Mess, who couldn't fit a hat over her bird's nest. We had determined looks around our mouths. We were all geared up.

I marched them down Irving Street past the YMCA, the library, and the shoemaker and over the bridge to the Wheatena factory, through the gate and right inside.

We startled a man sitting at the front desk chewing gum. He spit his gum out, as if he had been caught, and stuck it to the underside of the desk. I asked him where the packing floor was.

"What is it you want?"

"We want to see Mr. Reggio."

"Did he ask for you? I'll call up."

As he picked up the phone I shoved the others and we ran up the stairs. He took chase after us, but we were swift and found the office long before his huffing and puffing caught up.

"Are you Mr. Reggio?" I asked.

"Yes."

I put my hand out to shake his. "We've come to talk to you."

"Talk to me. Well, what would you lovely girls like?" He was bug-eyeing the Mess. "Come to see how Wheatena is made, see all those bags of grain from our heart land?"

"No," I said, "We have something much more important to discuss with you."

"Is that right?" He stood up so he could look down on The Mess's breasts.

"We're here to get"…I couldn't say The Indian. What was his name?

Glorybe jumped in, "My father. He was fired."

"Yes?"

"We want to get his job back."

I was real proud of her going forward.

"Is that right? And who are you, a delegation from the U.S. Congress?"

"That's not important," I said, I didn't want to say my name because of stirring up Mom's name.

"It isn't right to fire a man who has worked here fourteen years and has hardly missed a day," Selina said. She was also thinking of Jeremiah being fired by Mrs. Srickland.

"Is that right?" he said again in a tone like he meant to humiliate us.

"Yes." I tried to be polite. "That's right."

He thought a minute, looking at each of our faces and said, "You know what, you girls are right. Yessiree. As soon as somebody quits or good times come back we will consider hiring your father." He was mostly looking at the Mess and she knew it and slowly puffed out her chest.

"And I want to say you girls are brave and you look pretty enough for a parade, you sure do." He leaned over and pinched Bess-the-Mess's cheek and she swept his hand away like a fly. But he just grinned.

A whistle blew and he said, "Ah, Oh. I got to go to lunch now. That's the noon whistle so you beauties run along and play, nice to have seen you. Next time I'll show you around."

I planted my feet, "I'd like for you to put that into writing that when someone quits or things get better..."

"That's a good idea. I'll send you a letter." And then quick as a flash he began escorting us out the door and raced past us down the hall then turned before he disappeared and said, "Oh, stop at the front desk and they will give you each a box of Wheatena."

"We didn't win," Glorybe said.

Seeing her long face, I said. "In a way we did. I think he'll give him his job back..." I couldn't go on. She knew I was whistling in the dark. I put my arm around her. Of course we didn't stop at the desk to get the boxes of Wheatena. We hung around the parking lot for a few minutes, trying to sort out our failure.

"Were our mothers wrong?" Selina asked.

"Of course not," I said. But I wasn't sure. Maybe protests were of no use. I picked up a stick and dragged it along the sidewalk.

The Mess said, "We could try again soon."

Nobody answered her.

"I'm never eating Wheatena again," I said.

"But you never did," Selina said.

I found Mom that night and without telling her about the factory I asked her, "How do you go on doing more protests after you've failed, like with paving the Colored section?"

"Protests are like seeds. Some grow in the ground, some fail but little by little there are some that take hold."

"What if causes make things worse?"

"Nothing tried, nothing gained. You don't listen to *no*. You go right on.

"You have to be brave."

"Exactly."

I sat in contemplation and then said, "Will you comb my hair?"

She pulled a tortoise comb through my hair and my eyes half closed with the pleasure, not only of the combing but the scent of her, a mixture of ferns and apple blossoms.

CHAPTER 14

$\mathcal{I}$ tricked Annie, "So, you've never had a boyfriend have you?"

"Where did you get that idea?" Her nose turned pink.

"Then what's his name?"

"None of your business."

"So you're lying, you don't have one."

"The heck I don't. His name is Gordon Knight."

"Come on, that's a fake name."

"That's his name," Suzy said. She pinched her mouth with pride of knowing before I did.

"You dug him out of some dungeon?"

Annie was dying to spill it. "I met him at the train station."

"Do Mom and Dad know you hang around the crummy station?"

"Suzy had this dream I should. He commutes."

"He's a grown-up?"

"He's in college, in Boston. He has a summer job in a law office in Elizabeth."

"You just went up to him and started saying, I'd like to be your girl friend?"

"A damsel in distress," Suzy put in.

"Suzy had this great idea. I had my bike. I took some air out of the tire."

"You fooled him right off?"

"All is fair in love and war," Suzy said.

"So he pulled out his handy pump?" I asked.

Suzy's belly jiggled with laughter and Annie cupped her hand over her mouth.

"What's so funny?" I asked. But they didn't answer. They didn't have to because Jeremiah came in headed straight to my father. He had a sober look on his face and I rushed toward him and said quickly, sensing something wrong, "Want to play checkers later?"

"Not today, little one," Jeremiah said.

I stared at the door to Dad's study and wondered.

CHAPTER 15

"The mayor's son that awful Leland accosted Eliah," Dad said.

"What do you mean exactly?" Mom asked quickly.

"Leland told Eliah that he better tell Jeremiah he's not going to get away with it."

"Really?" Annie said, the first time she looked up from her dinner plate.

"What did Eliah say?" Mom asked.

Eliah didn't answer.

"But that worries me," Dad said, "with no witnesses that Jeremiah was home that night and the mayor will try his best to get Jeremiah in trouble instead of Leland, won't he? But I told Jeremiah they couldn't arrest him, with no evidence. They don't have the murder weapon, the knife. "

The first time I saw Jeremiah's knife close was the day he and Dad went out to the Meadowlands."

"Come on. Come on, Glorybe," I pleaded. Dad and Jeremiah will be back soon."

We ran to my stoop and waited.

"I'm not eating any." She wrinkled her nose.

"You don't even know what turtle tastes like."

"Neither do you."

"I don't have to know. Dad wouldn't be catching one if it wasn't wonderful.

Dad loves to cook. Mom doesn't believe in seasoning. She says food is best the way God made it. We try to keep her out of the kitchen."

"Who taught your dad?"

"My Grandma Davis. She asked Daddy to stay home from school when he was thirteen for half a year,'cause he was a grade ahead of himself and Grandma needed help with six younger kids. So she gave him frying up chicken lessons and Charlotte Russe lessons and Sally Lunn lessons and slimy okra and tomatoes lessons. Then Dad taught Suzy, but Suzy refused to make the okra."

"I've seen him racing around the kitchen, dripping stuff and then blowing off about his mistakes. He's like an elephant in a china shop."

I poked her one.

"I'm sorry. I didn't mean anything bad about your daddy. I really like him," Glorybe said, "a lot."

I didn't dare tell her, *not as much as I love your daddy.* Instead I said, "I don't know why they aren't here yet."

"Maybe a really big turtle pulled his boat over," she said. "And I heard bad men, like robbers, live out there in the Jersey meadows."

"Not funny," I said. "But if he had only taken my kayak..."

We put our chins on our knees and stared straight out. Annie came up the walk. "They've been out in the Meadowlands since dawn." she said, with an upset look.

Mom came out too. She paced up and down the driveway. I hated it when Mom was anxious. It was dark now. Glorybe and I stood in the road looking. We saw lights. But a car passed us, then another. The next car slowed down. When it swung into the driveway Jeremiah jumped out holding the biggest dead thing I'd ever seen. A turtle much bigger than any Thanksgiving turkey. It was glorious.

Dad said, "I'm sorry you were worried. The boat we rented got stuck on a sand bar. We had to step into the marsh and pull it loose. What are you holding your nose for? We smell as sweet as roses, don't we, Jeremiah?"

"You wouldn't have got stuck if you took me and my kayak."

"Maybe next time," he said. They couldn't go in the house until they got cleaned up under the hose and dried some. Now the huge turtle was in the kitchen sink, not moving. They had hit it over the head with a rock.

"We're going to make soup," Dad said.

That's when I saw it. Jeremiah slowly took out his fishing knife from the leather case on his belt. I couldn't help staring. It was the longest fishing knife I had ever seen. Pearl handled, beautiful and awful both. I shivered with wondering.

Could that be? No, it couldn't be. Jeremiah wasn't a murderer, even though he probably hated Strickland. No man I knew real well, no friend of mine would be a murderer.

Jeremiah leaned over the turtle and raised his arms and with one swipe whacked the dead turtle's head off. I gasped. His knife was that sharp. He held the body up to let the blood drip in the sink. Dad looked away. The sight of blood made him woozy.

Dad put on an apron. He looked silly because it covered only a little bit of him. He gave a bigger one to Jeremiah with printed daisies. But Dad didn't go to the sink. He was waiting for the blood to stop dripping.

Dad said, "First we boil Mr. Turtle. Glorybe, you get to drop him in." He was nice to my friends. Too nice, like now when I wanted to drop it in myself. But Glorybe pinched her lips with disgust and shut her eyes. We were all grinning at her as Jeremiah put the tail in her hand. The turtle was so heavy she had to let it splash into the huge kettle. Annie who was near the door for a moment left the room fast. She disliked anything slightly untidy. The four of us stood close watching the body bubble about with no head, even made *me* get the whim-whams.

"Okay," Dad said, taking his pocket watch out. "Time to pull her out and put her in the sink." He handed me two corn tongs. I had to hold tight and couldn't get a grip on the shell and then I did. Jeremiah helped me lift the turtle plop into the sink. I wondered if I would even taste it.

I decided Jeremiah would have shown something if he were bad enough to be a murderer. He would lie about other things. He would do more than cursing and a little gambling. Yet I stared at that big sharp knife, lying on the edge of the sink, dripping with blood. I took a deep breath to calm myself while also knowing he was very comfortable about slaughtering a turtle.

"First we scrub the nails," Jeremiah said. He handed a wire scrubber to both Glorybe and me. Glorybe shook her head, no, and went to lean against the refrigerator. The turtle's nails were as long as a bear's and thick and yellow. Then the legs. Jeremiah showed me how to scrub the legs. All the black scaly skin scrubbed off.

He picked up the legs one at a time and broke them, one at a time...not off, just broke them, snap. His hands were very strong. He picked up his knife and slid it under the shell, taking it off neat as a pin.

I made the chill about Jeremiah go away... I hoped forever. Mom always told me, "You're in control of your thoughts. Nobody else."

Jeremiah cut the turtle open so fast my eyes hardly caught it. He named each thing, "Liver, heart, gall bladder, never break that one."

"What would happen?" I asked.

"Horrible tasting things would come out of the gall bladder," Dad answered.

"Can I do the guts?" I asked. I wanted to take out my knife.

"Sure," Dad said, even though he didn't like me having a knife.

I was bold. I did it. I cut them and scooped them out with a spoon, sort of like scooping the innards out of a Halloween pumpkin. Threads and ribbons of guts. It was glorious. And Jeremiah washed his knife in the sink and I followed his example.

I got the nerve up. "Where did you get your knife?"

He looked surprised, like why was I asking but without hesitating he answered. "I saw it walking all alone down the street and gave it a home on my belt."

I felt ashamed of myself.

The soup was done. Jeremiah held a spoon for me to taste.

"Delicious," I said. I held the spoon out to Glorybe.

She paused, and paused some more, and finally tasted it and said, "Wow, it is delicious."

Jeremiah's eyes shone at her, and Dad gave her a big smile. I watched Jeremiah put the knife in the holder. At that moment it just seemed like an ordinary knife.

"Go run and get Easter and Eliah and Selina," Dad said. "I'll call your mother, Suzy and Annie. And Glorybe I'll save some in a pot for your dad, mom and brother.

Out the door Glorybe and I ran, down the road and over the bridge to Haydock Street.

Later, sitting around the table that night we were all happy, as if that would last, thinking it would last. We all held hands around the table when Jeremiah said the blessing and Dad said,"Amen."

And Easter said, "God has blessed us."

CHAPTER 16

"People will pay us to see them?"

"Wouldn't you?" I asked. "We have to try everything."

"Sure," Glorybe said, sounding doubtful. "Where are they?"

I took her into the back entry of my house to show her.

After he operated last year I had asked Dr. Rich if I could keep them. He left the room being noncommittal but when I woke up he presented me with a gift wrapped up like a Christmas present. I tore it open and there in a jar of formaldehyde were my tonsils.

Mom made me keep them on the shelf where Dad kept his tools. I reached up. I could feel nothing. Nothing was there. They weren't there on the shelf. I climbed on a chair. They were gone. I stormed back into the kitchen. "Suzy, where are my tonsils?"

"Here." She touched her throat.

"No, mine in the jar."

"What jar?"

"Stop yelling at her," Annie said, rising out of her chair. "I threw them out."

"No, you didn't. You wouldn't do that."

"They were totally disgusting."

"They were mine." I started to hit her but she grabbed my wrists. I broke loose and cuffed her on her head. She hit me back on my chin and we were holding on like prizefighters propelling each other into the stove and icebox and counters, when Suzy rushed in at us. And Mom came running.

Annie hollered in my ear, "I couldn't bring Gordon Knight here when he might discover them. How could I say, oh those, twerpy little floating balls are my sister's tonsils? He'd think you were nuts, that all of us were nuts and that would be the end."

"We need them to make money for The Indian."

"What?"

I stamped my feet. "Give them back. Where did you put them? I'm going to call the police. Robber. You took part of my body."

"What did you do with them, Annie?" Mom asked.

"I dumped them."

"Where?" I screamed.

"In the garbage."

"Get them out." I rushed to punch Annie again. Mom stood in the way.

"The garbage has been collected," Annie said.

"That was bad, Annie," Mom said. "You could have asked Theodora to take them to her room."

"I will hate you the rest of my life," I screamed at Annie.

Mom took my arm. "Hold on. It's terrible. They were yours and Annie had no right and she will be punished."

"It's worth it," Annie said and rushed upstairs.

"They were part of me," I hollered after her. "How could you take something that was part of me and throw them away? Murderer! You are probably the one who murdered Mr. Strickland."

"Wow, almost sounds like my house," Glorybe said.

Annie called down, "Getting rid of those will make you get a boyfriend too, when you want one, some day. Throwing the tonsils away is sort of magic. They were what you had when you were a child and now you are going to be grown-up soon."

"Wow," Glorybe said again."

But I thought, who would love me? I was too ugly. My hair was brown, not blond like Annie, my eyes were green not blue. I was a bad speller and she was good. I felt soggy with tears.

I wanted everything to change. But I didn't want anything to be different because wouldn't that mean all the old things I loved would be gone? I rocked back and forth. You're not getting away with this, Annie, I vowed.

CHAPTER 17

$\mathcal{I}$ think she knew I could be lethal. I was almost as tall as Annie now.

We had avoided each other for a day or two but out of the blue she said in a secretive voice, "I'll show you something."

"No."

"Follow me," she whispered, "I'll teach you something."

"I don't want you teaching me anything."

She started out the back door. I waited but couldn't resist. Annie was going to do something with me. She was letting me in on something. "Teaching me what?" I was suspicious it was a trick, and flattered to death.

"You'll see. Go get Glorybe, she can come too."

I called for Glorybe. The Indian wasn't there. Then he appeared and slowly moved to lie down in the hammock, his cheekbones looked as if they would burst through his pale skin. "Hi," I said, hoping he didn't notice my face filled with distress.

"I'm not feeling okay these days," he said and his eyes stayed on my eyes; he was telling me something without words. Was he telling me he wanted to stay on this earth and be with me or was he just sleepy and tired. My heart listed to one side. He collapsed into the hammock and went into spasms of coughing. Glorybe came rushing to bring him a drink of water.

"We called the doctor," she said. They'd only had a doctor in their house once before when her brother had cut his arm something awful falling on broken glass in the baseball field.

"You two go play," the Indian said to Glorybe. "I'm okay."

I wanted to stay with him longer.

"Go," he said. He closed his sunken river-colored eyes.

"Come on," Glorybe said.

I hesitated before I moved. I couldn't talk for a moment.

As we walked I said, "We'll get some cash somehow."

We followed Annie out to the chicken coop. She looked around to be sure nobody was watching. "Take your knife," she said to me. I still couldn't believe she was bringing me in on some secret and I still wondered if there were treachery behind it. Glorybe was all a twitter too. We were standing under the grape arbor where it was very shady. Annie cut a narrow piece of vine. Then she cut that in three pieces. "Glance down the middle. What do you see?"

"Light," I said.

"Open your mouths."

She put one in each of our mouths and one in hers. She pulled out matches from her skirt pocket and lit one on a rock. Then she lit the ends of the vines, "This is your first cigarette. Draw, Slowly."

But I dragged too fast. Burning flames rushed down my throat. I dropped the vine.

"It does burn a little," Annie agreed. "Great, huh?"

"Great," I lied, swallowing and swallowing.

"It was just an experiment," Annie said. "I never did this before."

"Not a good experiment. My throat hurts a little too," Glorybe said, but I knew she hadn't dragged on the vine at all.

"We can wash it down with Coca Cola," Annie said.

"What do you mean Coca Cola?" I whispered. I held my throat. We were never allowed soda in our house. But Annie had some hidden under the lilac bush. We guzzled.

Annie said, "Next time, real cigarettes."

"Yeah," I answered. I loved Annie again.

Dad said, "You better stay in bed."

I couldn't tell him why my throat was sore. I had just asked him for aspirin. Mom was having an integrated meeting hoping to scout out new projects.

"I will only stay in bed if you tell me farm stories, like tell me about the slaughtering time."

He gave me a drink of water. "I was just your age when your grandpa said, 'It's your turn to learn and led me to the barn. My older brothers had slaughtered but I'd never even wanted to watch."

"Father brought the lamb into the barn, dragging it away from its mother."

Dad paused and began pacing the floor, which of course he liked to do when he was looking for a strong signal from God in preparing his sermons.

"Father brought the lamb to the edge of the barn where the large wooden doors were open and forced the creature down, hanging its head over the edge so the blood would run down the ditch. Father said, 'Hold the lamb's legs, Chester.' I knelt down and held the warm legs as the lamb struggled and kicked at me and then your grandpa raised his knife and with his other hand held the lamb's chin up as it baaed and baaed. Then he brought his knife to its throat and..."

"And what?"

"I fainted. I woke up outside the barn in the grass with Father standing over me and stroking my head. I looked up at him. 'I never want to do that again,' I said.

'You'll never have to, son,' he answered."

"Grandpa was a nice man," I said.

"Yes, he was. But I didn't really tell him why I had fainted. It was not just that he was slaughtering an animal, or that there was blood. It was because I thought of what Jesus was called."

"The Lamb of God..." I broke in.

"Exactly, I felt as if I were holding Jesus' head over the ditch and Father was slicing his throat. Even though I knew, of course, thinking of Jesus as the lamb was just symbolic, like our communion grape juice is symbolic for the blood of Jesus."

"Jesus' head over a ditch." I shivered. "That's why you don't want Suzy serving lamb. But the symbol of communion which is drinking his blood, isn't that like being a cannibal?"

"The symbolic meaning is something like this: if you truly understand another person you'll take his flesh into yourself and take his blood into yourself. In other words to feel exactly what he feels, his troubles, his sadness. That's what it symbolizes."

"So when Jesus died on the cross it was to make us know other people's sadness."

"Yes, that's it. You understand."

"What about their happiness? Is Jesus only interested in sadness?"

"He loves most of all for us to be happy. But really deep happiness comes from understanding and helping others."

"That's why you're going to bring me chocolate candy as soon as you can."

Dad smiled and patted my cheek.

Later that day Eliah came by to say his father would come after supper to mow the lawn. That was later than usual. I looked at him carefully. You have a bruise on your cheek. At first he didn't want to say why. And then he said that Leland and his brother found him walking to his house and told him this time, your father is going to jail. Eliah said back, the hell he is. You know perfectly well who the murderer is. Leland wanted to date Strickland's daughter and he wouldn't let him. Then a fight started. The mayor's two kids beat up Eliah.

After Eliah left Mom and Dad were talking. "This is very disturbing. Not good. Anything could happen. It's not the south. Those boys are pretty evil."

"I'm afraid," I said.

They looked at me saying nothing.

Chapter 18

As Mom and I were leaving for down town to buy fabric for my school dress, I hear this familiar voice saying hello, which made me cringe.

There was nothing else to do but stop and speak to Miss Ethel and Miss Edith Jardine who had been my first and second grade teachers. Old maids we called them in those days.

"Theodora," Miss Ethel Jardine said, "Didn't I see you with those Colored kids in the river?"

"What is your point?" Mom said, quick as a flash.

They loved to tell tales on the minister's kid. Everything fun was naughty to them.

"I've been hearing things about--you know," Miss Edith said, moving her head like a ball bearing.

"And what could that be?" Mom asked.

I disliked them both the same. On my report card Miss Edith wrote, "Theodora is very imaginative." And she meant it as an insult.

"I hear it's quite likely, those Colored children's father..."

"Excuse me." Mom said, "What exactly are you trying to say?"

I hated their around-Robin-Hood's-barn approach.

"I've seen him gambling with marbles and getting hot under the collar," Miss Edith said.

"Gambling," Miss Ethel said, her eyes themselves bulgy as marbles.

"So I play marbles too." I said to her.

"I've seen this particular man's temper rise," Miss Ethel said.

"Your temper never rose?" Mom asked, knowing how she could yell up a storm at her class.

Miss Edith wrinkled her nose. "Well, you know, the mayor, I mean since the... has been getting at crime, like looking into certain sections of town, if you get my meaning. It's okay when the dark side stays down on H...Street, but when it comes uptown, get my meaning, that's a different kettle of fish."

"What's a kettle of fish had to do with it?" Mom said to them. "I think you better spill what's on your mind."

Miss Ethel leaned toward Mom's ear. "Mr. Strickland is dead."

"I know that. Spill out your dirty prejudice."

Miss Edith drew a breath of surprise at my mother. "The reason could be a friend of yours."

"You have no right," Mom said.

"It's not us talking. It's a lot of folks."

Mom took my arm and moved away from them, not even saying, good day, to them. She walked so fast I could hardly keep up.

"Is Jeremiah going to be arrested?"

"Not if I have anything to do with it."

That wasn't too comforting.

CHAPTER 19

My sister slipped through the hedge, leaving for town. "Look at that," I said.

"Annie has changed into the movie star, Veronica Lake." Her hair completely covered one eye and swept down the side of her nose. She washed her hair every day now to make it glossy and thick as corn silk. And she had to shake it every five seconds so you'd notice. I worried that one eye would go blind from hair covering it all the time.

"Her room," I said to Glorybe, and we raced for the house.

Annie's wallpaper was a beautiful blue with a yellow pattern of red Japanese lanterns. She and Mom had gone to New York to pick it out. "It's from France," she crowed. She had paid for it from baby-sitting, which she hated and claimed she wouldn't think of having children of her own. Aunt Florence had made her a quilt covered with blue and red squares to match the paper. She made me a quilt of diamond shapes with every color in the rainbow. I know Annie thought mine was tacky but I didn't care.

Annie's room was super neat, neat on the outside, a spewed volcano on the inside so we could easily mess around and she'd never know.

"Where did she get the desk?"

"Grandpa Logan. He owned a flourmill and invented white flour. When he made too much he used it to mulch his tomatoes."

"Oh sure."

The desk was practically the only piece of furniture in our house that wasn't borrowed or given by the congregation and most were on their last legs. The desk was mahogany through and through, not veneer, Annie liked to explain to her friends. We rummaged quickly. But we only came up with stuff like paper, paper clips and pencils. "Her bureau drawers," I whispered.

Our hands fumbled under her underwear. "Look at this." found a picture. "A boy, no, a man." We stared. He had a wide face and thick hair and eyes that slanted in the corners, one seemed half closed. His lips were pouty and slightly parted, "As if he were about to whisper lovey-dovey words," I said.

His head was thrown back and he was glancing to one side. "La-de-da, her boyfriend," I said.

"Look, what's this?" I undid sheets of paper held together with a crisscross of ribbons. The first page said, "Today it happened. We were walking under the railroad bridge. Nobody was around. We leaned against the tree. Rather I leaned against the tree and he bent toward me, his whole chest against mine, his whole mouth surrounding my whole mouth. Hours went by."

"Hours? They don't even kiss that long in the movies," Glorybe said.

"But Annie doesn't lie except when she tells my parents I've done something bad."

"Wow, kissing that long. Does your neck get stiff?"

"I think you don't care if your neck gets stiff," I said.

We flipped through the pages fast, but the rest were empty. We put the diary back. We sat on her quilt, staring at each other in glee, like we'd discovered the North Pole or something.

"What kind of husband do you want?" Glorybe asked.

I pressed my lips, pretending I'd never thought about that. "You first."

"He has got to be tall, tall as your Daddy. Six feet. He's got to be funny, like your daddy or the butcher when he shows off with his big cleaver and cuts a hunk of meat right in half and yells, whoops, like he'd chopped his finger right in half."

"Yeah?" I paused but had to tell her. "I want my husband to look like your dad and dance like your dad."

"Yeah?" She smiled. Thank God she didn't pause on that.

"And I want my husband to look like Graham Harwood."

"The coach?" I screamed.

"No, his son, silly." We threw ourselves backward on the bed because our giggling bodies wouldn't hold us up…the thought of Glorybe loving the coach, with his no hair, his double chin, breath like a locomotive, severely tobacco stained teeth and scowly lips he sucked in until they disappeared when he got mad.

I drew in a gasp because I just thought of the horrible dream I had about Weiggle but of course I couldn't mention that. He was chasing me by the river, then into the river and over the rocks, and then deep into the river and the river was warm and lapping and glorious. Then he caught me, rolling me around in the water. I tried to scream but he pulled me against him and pressed his lips right on my lips. It was disgusting and something else, like Suzy spooning some muck on my plate and Mom making me taste it and finding, gosh, it was wonderful. I was ashamed to death of the dream. And I wondered why I had dreamt that the devil kissed me right on the mouth when I had never dreamt that Jesus kissed me right on the mouth.

CHAPTER 20

"Look at that. There's somebody sleeping in the church window well."

"Let's go closer," Glorybe said.

"This could be God's plan. God put him there for us to get Lucifer's goat?" She loved it when I called Weiggle different names like Lucifer, Beelzebub or fiend.

"Why get Lucifer's goat? Why not his cow or his horse?"

"Glorybe, you're a screwball."

"Don't a lot of tramps come to your house begging for something to eat?"

"Sure, but they don't stay around so you can talk to them."

"Look," she whispered.

He was all curled up in the dry leaves.

"How old do you think?" I whispered.

"Who's going to wake him up?"

"Let's both of us."

We found a little branch from the dying elm tree. First I poked him gently and then she poked him. We waited. He jerked his head up. I jumped. Maybe he'd harm us. But, wow, he wasn't much older than us.

He sat up. "What the hell do you crows want?"

"How old are you?" I asked.

"You wake me up to ask me how old I am? I got to make myself a don't disturb sign."

We laughed. But we couldn't tell if he thought that was funny.

"So?" I asked again.

"So, it's none of your business."

"Well," I said, crossing my arms over my chest, "This is my father's church."

"Yeah, what's his name, Jesus Christ?"

"Both of them own it," Glorybe explained.

"Can I go back to sleep now?"

"Have you run away?" Glorybe asked.

"The other way around," he said. "My old man and lady up and left me by the side of the road. They thought I was old enough to be on my own. I'm fourteen. They didn't want to feed me anymore."

"Wow," I said. "Are you hungry?"

"What do you think?"

"We'll bring you some food."

He almost smiled. I wondered what he'd look like if his blond hair was washed.

We didn't tell my parents. We sneaked past Daddy's study window and under the window of Miss Shrimp's office, that was his secretary, so neither one of them would see our arms full of stuff, a mayonnaise jar and a cooked chicken, two pickles and

Suzy's lemon pie that got smashed a little from the napkin we used to cover it.

My parents didn't have much money either so they might be mad about the chicken. Usually Suzy made a sandwich for the tramps who came knocking at our door.

I never saw anybody eat like that. He didn't even take time to crawl out of the window well. He dipped the spoon in the mayonnaise jar and gobbed it into his mouth, scooped some over and over in between eating hunks of chicken. I held my belly wondering what it was like to be that hungry.

"You got a beer?" he asked.

"My mom does," Glorybe offered. She was gone. She knew just where she kept the supply behind the sofa.

"What does your old man drink, whiskey?" he asked me.

I sort of shrugged my shoulders. I thought of communion. "He drinks blood once in a while." I wished we could be like everybody else and have real booze around.

"Does he get drunk on blood and beat you up?"

"What else?"

"Terrible, ain't it?"

"Like hell," I said and I tried to feel it.

Glorybe came back with the beer and we sat next to him on the grass. "Want to have a neat place to sleep tonight?" I asked.

He guzzled his beer and nodded.

"We'll show you how to sneak in the church. You'll be nice and cool there and you can sleep on a pew and take the food in. There is a cushion and we'll bring you more stuff to eat and you can leave the garbage for the janitor to clean up. He likes cleaning up." Glorybe and I eyed each other.

When we left Glorybe and I were singing our song, "The devil has taken God's church. The devil is sweeping the floor. The devil is vacuuming scrubbing and polishing. The devil be gone. The devil be gone."

But it was the boy who was gone the next day when we rushed into the church. "Glorybe, look at the great mess he left." We clapped our hands and ran out quickly. He had left chicken bones and part of a pickle and prune pits and an empty beer bottle. It was glorious.

"But we don't even know his name. We didn't find out where he went. We didn't know anything more about him and we'll probably never see him again, not ever in our whole lives," I said.

I imagined for weeks afterward what he would look like all cleaned up. I even wondered what he'd be like to kiss. That, I think, was the first time I had met somebody and never saw him again. That made me ponder, as when I was in the kayak, how ephemeral life was, and a sharp pain came, thinking of The Indian.

When I bounced in the kitchen door Dad was waiting with a serious face. Suzy had reported the missing chicken and the pie.

"I don't know anything about it," I said and started to rush away. But Dad caught my arm.

"Theodora, I don't want you ever lying, you know that."

"Yes." But that was all I said and that was all Dad said.

When he left I stuck my tongue out at Suzy.

CHAPTER 21

*E*arly in the morning, the sun already scorching the August sky and my feet leathery tough by then, I thought I would call for Glorybe, thought we'd crayfish, thought we could take them all to the Indian, who stayed in bed all the time now. I couldn't bear it. He was on my mind all day long. And maybe we could think up another way to make money.

The first death of someone you love leaves a gorge of a scar on your heart, although new layers of love help dim the scar. But even with years of happiness you remember the anguish, my mother told me when I was grown. That was when she expressed her terrible grief over losing my brother and before then seeing their beloved servant lynched.

That was how I felt, like death was whispering at me, as I climbed Glorybe's steps and the hammock was not there. The house looked dead. Glorybe never slept this late. Blinds were shut like closed eyes. The screen door was moaning as it swung in the heat-shimmering breeze. When I knocked on the door, it was my heartbeat knocking, hard, harder, fast, faster.

The silence went so deep I couldn't find the bottom. Where were they? I looked in a window and the living room looked as if every personal possession of theirs had been swept away, even the radio with the snapping doors.

I plunked down on the top step, not knowing what to do. What should I do? I was spinning around on the sidewalk, looking everywhere as if she would suddenly appear. That's when Weiggle came along holding the leash of one of his ugly dogs." What's the matter?" he said, trying to smile, but like he wasn't used to pulling his lips to the sides.

I didn't answer.

"You looking for Gloria?"

I nodded.

He said, "They moved in the night. I heard they didn't have the rent money and were evicted."

"Where. Where?"

"I don't know."

Frantically I knocked at the next door neighbor.

The woman I had rarely seen answered and told me, to go three doors down they might know.

I rushed down the block and knocked loudly. Waited. Knocked again. An old man I hardly knew answered. "Yes?"

"I'm looking for Gloria."

"They moved."

"Do you know where?"

"I believe Berwin Street."

Thank God they hadn't moved out of town.

I got on my bike, sped on the bumpy sidewalk and nearly ran over a cat. Berwin Street was almost as bad as where Jeremiah's family lived. I asked a woman with no teeth if she knew where Gloria lived and she pointed to a house that looked sad enough to collapse.

I knocked on the warped door. Nobody answered and finally Glorybe opened the door a crack. She didn't say anything.

"You moved."

"We had to."

My face flushed with anger. "How could you move without telling me? We are best friends."

"I can't be friends anymore."

"If you're friends, you're friends. There is no such thing as anymore."

"Shuu, my father is asleep." She lowered her eyes.

"Are you going to ask me in?"

"No."

"Why not? Is your mother here?"

"She's out looking for a job. I have to get a job."

"Are you going to invite me in?"

She stayed put. I pushed by her.

"This place is awful, isn't it?" She asked.

"You think that matters to me? What kind of a person do you think I am? I don't care where you live."

My eyes had to adjust in the dark and my nose to the dank, cloying room, a sweetness that is the smell of a dying flower... dustier, far drearier than her other house, then any place I'd ever been. Worse than the grimness of the church tower...how frightened she must have been to eat and go to bed there. My eyes cleared and I saw that the place consisted of only a room, where stood a table, four chairs, a rocker and a pullout bed that was still open and with a deep swale in the middle.

"You and your mother sleep there?"

"Like sleeping with a squishy toad."

I began to laugh. The two of us doubled over.

I looked around for The Indian when I heard a cough. He was in an alcove off the small kitchen where curtains were thrown across a rod for privacy. I wanted to go see him immediately but I was also shy and of course I had come empty-handed. Instead I asked, "Where does your brother sleep?"

"Over there." She pointed to a floppy worn mildewed chair. "He says he doesn't mind. He works. He's the only one that brings groceries home. He works for Ansiers, cleaning up and at six A.M. he is a paper boy, throwing the papers up on the porches."

"I'll give you some of my allowance."

She tried to say, thank you, but she was choking up.

"Can I say hi to your father?"

She led me to the curtain and pulled it back. "Daddy, Theodora is here to say hi."

All feeling had rushed from my legs to my heart. His face was the white of carved stone, his nose a sharp point, his cheeks sunken and his dark eyes seemed so immobile they looked carved in stone also. It was difficult as a child to believe what you desired to act upon would be socially acceptable. I wanted to take his hand and hold it but thought that wouldn't be right. The shock on my face must have jolted him into saying, "The horseman hasn't come for me yet. I'm going to get well." He paused, but didn't go on.

"Glorybe and I are going to get more crayfish for you."

"Are you? That will stir up the old blood, Theodora, minister's kid."

"Yes," I whispered. I couldn't move.

Lying up in bed that night, the heat rising and stifling me, the sheets a sticky and crumpled, my awful thoughts ran like our raging river covering me with suffocating plumes of water...what if The Indian stopped breathing? What if his eyes stopped seeing me, or his lips stopped rushing out his Lenni Lenape songs?

What if Gruber put him in a white coffin with his turquoise bracelets and I and Glorybe lay the feathers, we had gathered, over his coffin and Gruber rolled him into the black hearse, the one I was born in, and he would never move again?

What if Mom said she wouldn't make me a black dress for the funeral because I was too young? And then I persuaded her because I'd cry so loud and she would see that my heart was cut in two. And of course I would check the seams to be sure there was enough fabric that they wouldn't pull loose.

Glorybe's mother would be out of her apron for the first time in my life and Glorybe's brother would be wearing a jacket that Gruber lent him and Glorybe would be in a black straw hat and heels that the Mess lent her, and I'd be in Annie's heels and Glorybe would stare straight ahead, like sleep walking.

Her family would be bundled together, holding each other up, all of them blind, I would be blind too, because my eyes would be swimming under water. I would never see The Indian again. How could that be true?

The neighbors would be there and Jeremiah's family wiping their eyes and Dad's crying would not embarrass me for the first time in my life.

CHAPTER 22

$\mathcal{I}$ wanted Jeremiah to tell me something so I asked him to play checkers after he worked. For the moment there was no more talk about him and the murder. For the moment. We sat under the huge sycamore tree and Suzy was nice that day and brought us lemonade. Jeremiah, will you tell me about heaven like you did that time. I was thinking that at least The Indian and I might be together there.

"Heaven." He stirred the ice in the drink with his finger. "When you get to heaven everybody lines up by a huge white table, as long as a football field, laid out with roast beef, sliced and rare as snow in June. And when you bite down the juice runs right out the corners of your mouth and onto hammered gold plates. I only tasted roast beef like that once in my life at my cousin's house at Christmas.

"Then when you get your full, up you rise and dance...dance like from dawn and all morning, all day, all night till your calves ache, dance till your head falls forward and then falls back, dance till your shoulders fold in and your knees turn to water."

"Indian dancing?"

"You'd like that Theodora?"

I blushed.

"Every kind of dancing. Rumba, Charleston, waltz."

"But how do they see? Isn't it dark?"

"No," he laughed. "There is no darkness in God's heaven. The honey of God's light shafts down upon you, light as wide as the river at Perth Amboy. Light as tall as the church tower." He raised his arm into a circle.

"Yessir, God gives you light and you carries it in your innards and you carries the light in your eyes and when you sleep a ring of light showers you with fairness and drifts you through meadows as yellow as corn and with waving light similar to tinsels of wheat... deep into meadows, meadows of the soul. It is you that becomes illumination, glowing with happiness."

Jeremiah stood up.

"But what do you breathe?"

He rocked back and forth and sang his words like the preacher in his church. "Ah, the sweetness of the air, sweeter than magnolias or roses, or honeysuckle, sweeter than blooming locust, or bursting lilacs..."

He paused and thought, like he was seeing something far off and his voice changed into greater solemnity. "Heaven, in heaven there is no such thing as Colored people. No, no Colored people of any kind, no dark people, or yellow or red or bronze."

"Why is that?"

He smiled, showing his crowded large teeth. "Every human being and every animal, cat and dog and all them song birds are the same color."

"The same color? What? Like blue or green?"

"Gold, gold as can be. No more black and no more white and no more yellow and no more red. And there are no long sad faces. Yet, you don't got to smile all the time neither, or pretend you are happy, 'cause there is no other state to be in. But the biggest thing of all, Theodora..."

"Yes?"

"Is that in heaven there is no fear. No fear lurking in the shadows, or pumping in your heart. There is only love. God's love comes down on you soft as spring moss."

"Only love," I repeated.

"You don't have to grow love alone, neither, all by yourself, you don't have to chase after it. It's like a lake, an ocean or like air. Love is what you breathe."

I held my hands together.

He let his eyelids fall and whispered, "And in heaven the reason you don't got to smile all the time?"

This part was new to me. He hadn't mentioned this before.

"Smiling comes from fear. Smilin' comes from you needing the other person to know that you are no threat, when just about everybody on this earth is a threat to somebody else, one time or another."

"Really? I never thought of that." Was it true? I frowned.

He opened his black eyes at me. He looked the most serious I had ever seen him. "Theodora, living is fear. We got to go on living with fear attached to us like it's our very legs and arms. But it's more important than a leg or an arm. Yes, fear is the best thing you can have on earth when the worst black clouds comes down hard on you. Fear gives you the might that says, don't never lie down. No sir, don't you *never lie down.*"

115

That night when all the lights were out I pictured heaven. But I couldn't figure out about the bodies. Weren't they all skeletons? Did God take them up to heaven and put flesh back on them? Did he ever get mixed up, like put the wrong skin on the wrong bones so you had Grandma's leg flesh put on the heavy bones of Grandpa and then it didn't cover all the way so there might be spots with the leg bone sticking out? Please God if The Indian dies, please put him back together right...so when I see him... "

CHAPTER 23

"Come on, my brothers are all out. This will work," Bess-the-Mess said. She had nine brothers. I would have liked to have a bunch of brothers.

I asked Dad once why there were only two of us and why the Mess had so many. Dad said that was because they were Catholic and liked a lot of kids.

"Protestants don't like kids?"

"Yes, they do. Of course," Dad said. "They just believe in control."

"Controlling what?"

"Controlling's not the exact word, limiting."

"Limiting in what way?"

He thought a minute. "Limiting smart-alecks like you."

"Daddy," I screeched.

Bess-the-Mess's lived in the wealthier part of town. The house rambled with a lot of wings and even a turret on top with a widow's walk where the wives watched for their men to come home from the sea. But why was it on her house when you couldn't see anything but the shallows of the Rahway River?

We climbed the deep red newly painted steps onto the deep red newly painted porch. "Did your dad paint this with the blood of the animals?" I teased. Her father was a butcher.

Glorybe and Selina and I laughed and even the Mess laughed.

"Two of my brothers painted, bitching the whole time. All they want to do is rev up and roar their motorcycles and make us crazy."

"All nine of them got motorcycles?" Selina asked.

"Yep, gigantic ones. But Kevin is getting married and his girl friend wants a Chevy."

We were inside taking our shoes off to climb the curved stairs to the second floor, holding onto the thick mahogany railing. The stairs were the only cleared spot in the house. The rooms were stuffed with furniture, like a furniture store. The living room had two pianos, both white, that the Mess said nobody played. Her parents just liked the looks of them.

I thought carpeting was on the strangest places, like the stairs and the halls. My bare feet felt as if I were tramping on a fairy glen. Selina went up and down the steps twice just to feel the softness. "You sure your mother won't be back?" Glorybe asked.

"Don't worry, she's gone to work at the beauty parlor."

"My mother doesn't get permanents; she curls hers with an iron," I said.

"How can an iron curl your hair?" the Mess asked.

"A curling iron, silly."

We all laughed.

Selina said, "My mother puts stuff on to uncurl her hair."

"Why do your father's waves always look so good?" Glorybe asked me.

"After his shower he takes my mother's old stocking, cuts it in half and ties a knot to make this incredibly silly cap. The cap keeps his hair from waving too much because he's embarrassed when people exclaim over his gorgeous hair."

"I gave two of my little brothers permanents," the Mess said. "But I didn't read the directions right and a lot of their hair fell out."

"Weren't they hopping mad?" Selina asked.

"Mom was mad. But she's mad at me all the time anyways. I think she wishes I was a boy."

"She wants ten boys?" Selina asked.

"What if she catches us in her room?" Glorybe asked.

"We jump out the window."

I went to the window to look way down on the cement driveway.

She opened the closet with three doors that folded out into three mirrors like a fancy department store. I loved how I could see all of my back and front and the magic of many many of me.

The Mess kept pulling out the dresses and furs. I'd never seen such an expensive wardrobe as that. I put on a pale green dress.

"Look at how skinny my legs are," I shouted in horror.

"Look at my face, I'm a hawk," Glorybe said.

"My breasts are two different sizes," Selina squealed.

"One must have had better nourishment than the other," The Mess said.

"My breasts are as heavy as basketballs." They laughed since I hardly had apricot sized ones. But I didn't care because I disliked big breasts since I had a third grade teacher who used to run her hands down inside her blouse and feel her enormous breasts while teaching. Just about the whole class got bad grades. We couldn't concentrate.

"Let's measure ours."

The mess was enthusiastic and rummaged to find a tape measurer but only found a yardstick.

"That's no good," Glorybe said, rolling her eyes at me.

"We could at least try," The Mess said.

We tore off our blouses and I started on The Mess. "Two inches up, two across."

Selina measured Glorybe. "One inch up and two across."

The Mess measured Selina.

"Wow." We looked. "four inches out and four across."

"Impressive," I said.

I was really embarrassed over mine. Glorybe measured. "One half an inch up and not much across."

"Don't worry, they will grow," The Mess said. "Particularly if you feel them a lot."

"You win the prize," I said to Selina. There before us was something magnificent...something you might see years later in Playboy magazine, luscious- proud and round as melons.

"Okay we got to hurry."

"Zip me up," Glorybe asked. She had on a slinky black velvet evening gown. She waved her arms so as not to get wet armpits.

"Here's perfume," the Mess sprayed our hair and neck. "Oops, almost used up the bottle and Mom has to send to Paris for more."

"Wow," Glorybe said when the Mess put on a risqué lacy pink dress. She then put on a white silk coat and over her shoulder a fur animal with beads for eyes. I thought she might suffocate in the heat.

Selina put on a gold lame' evening gown that she had to hold up so the hem wouldn't drag. That's about when we heard Bess-the-Mess's mother. We tumbled out of the room, down the back steps to the kitchen. Out the back door. Down the driveway. We got away. I still had to zip up my green silk dress.

Out on the street we looked at one another. We were great looking. The Mess had put our hair up in knots. We looked like an ad for hair spray.

The dresses were very loose and the shoes with high heels didn't quite fit, but we had stuffed them with newspapers.

Glorybe and The Mess and Selina and I had to walk slowly to the house where Mrs. Brown and the cousins lived and people stared because we were so beautiful.

Bess-the-Mess said, "Let me do the talking. I'm experienced."

Mrs. Brown was older than Mom so she sagged, breasts and belly. But I liked her looks, even her wispy mustache. When in the yard she sang, *Beer Barrel Polka* over and over, like it was her only song. Sometimes she swore as she puttered around the dirt yard. I liked that too.

She talked about things Mom never talked about like the kind of floor mop she hankered after or what kind of soap she used in the wash. Sometimes she let me help her hang the cousins' underwear. I never saw underwear like that, pongee, red or black or gold, sometimes with triangles of lace.

The cousins weren't always the same ones. They came and went. Some of them smiled and were nice to me, but they didn't come down in the dirt yard. Just stayed on the porch until their dates came to call on them.

Mrs. Brown answered the door. She was still in her nightie though it was mid-afternoon and her hair was up in curlers and she had a bandanna on and she was holding a pot of coffee. "Theodora, is that you all dressed up?" She looked like she was going to laugh. But she wouldn't laugh, I said to myself. We looked beautiful, didn't we?

The Mess stepped in front of me. She put her hand out to shake Mrs. Brown's hand. "How are you?"

"Fine, Bess, how are you?" She smiled back, real broad.

"Could we step into your parlor?" The Mess said, arching her eyebrows that she had darkened so much they looked like a raccoon's.

"How about the kitchen," Mrs. Brown said.

"Very good," I said, wobbling forward on the high heels.

But as we all followed the Mess whispered into my ear, "I'm afraid the kitchen doesn't make us look important."

Glorybe overheard and put her head up high. And Selina had a proud smile like our mothers on their protests. I peeked in the parlor and saw more cushions and chaise lounges and tufted pillows than I had ever seen in any living room and everything was maroon or dark purple, even the walls. There were red-fringed lampshades on the lamps. It all seemed so exotic I wanted to go right home and beg for a purple bedroom.

The three of us and Mrs. Brown sat at the kitchen table. She said, "Let's talk softly. The cousins are asleep. You all look very pretty. But she said that with a puzzled voice. "How about some coffee?" She then said, as if we were adults. I wasn't allowed any at home, but I drank it like a pro, allowing the bitter stuff to slide right down without making a face.

"So you walking around town being ladies today, huh? Look at those fancy dresses. Bess in a white silk coat, Gloria in black and Selina Johnson in gold and you that sea green and the fancy heels, and what make-up." She still had that about-to-double-over expression.

"We came to talk to you," Glorybe said with a serious expression. She was trying to be an adult.

"You see," the Mess broke in, "Gloria's father, you know, The Indian." She stopped. I could tell that a lot of saliva was under her tongue. "He can't work and is really sick and they need a doctor and we need to help him out. He lost his job and the way conditions are today…"

"Difficult to find…" Mrs. Brown was leaning on her elbows looking at each of our faces.

"And my dad lost one job he had also, so…" but Selina couldn't go on.

"I know," Mrs. Brown said with sympathy.

"We need a job," I said.

She looked carefully at each of us again. Something was flashing signals inside her brain. She was mulling it over.

"You want me to give you ideas? Or is it money? I guess you think I'm rich. You know bad times are everywhere, even here."

"Oh no," I rushed in…

The Mess said, "None of those things, really. We want to work like the cousins."

"Like the cousins?"

"Yes," Selina said, pushing her hair from her forehead. Mrs. Brown grew bigger and fatter all of a sudden. "And what kind of work do you think the cousins do? Theodora, is this your idea?"

"It's all of ours." I gulped. I didn't know what had upset her.

"What do you think the cousins do?"

Bess-the-Mess said, "They dress up and men come to..."

"That's enough," Mrs. Brown said.

"What *do* they do?" I asked, confused.

Mrs. Brown paused. She looked at each of us again. "No, you tell me what you think they do. I've changed my mind; I have to hear."

"I think the men come and pay to look at the beautiful girls," The Mess said.

"That's it?" She asked, like she was accusing us of something.

"That's it." The Mess said.

"Do you think we could get paid?" I asked.

"I'm afraid not."

"You don't think we're beautiful enough?" Glorybe asked softly.

Mrs. Brown was smiling kindly now. She even went to get us some cookies from her jar. She looked each of us one at a time. Glorybe had piles of lipstick on. The-Mess gave me a hat of real ostrich feathers. But my hair was coming loose at my ears.

"We really *need a job,*" Selina said, frowning.

"But..." Mrs. Brown paused, I think to find the right words. "I'm sorry...you're just not old enough."

"How old do you have to be?" I asked.

Her smile never let go. "You have to be at least ten years older." Then her voice changed, really kind and soft. "I won't tell your mommies. You shouldn't be dressing up in those good clothes and at your age and walking around, you should be out playing like kids in the sunshine and getting brown." She looked at Selina. " As brown as Selina, and having not a care..."

"But my daddy's sick," Glorybe said.

She took Glorybe's hand and I could tell she didn't have an answer to that so she just said, "I'm sorry, honey."

"She wasn't mean," Selina said.

"But she wasn't right," I said.

Bess-the-Mess offered us pop gum and we all took it. But the gum made our speaking fuzzy.

"Maybe the truth was she didn't think we were beautiful enough," Glorybe fuzzed out.

We'll practically be dead in ten years...twenty-three and twenty-four," The Mess said.

"Good for you, Bess," I said. "You added that in your head."

"I think we look wonderful," Glorybe said this time.

"Look how everybody up and down the street is staring at us."

I wished I could think of something else we could do. I took Glorybe's hand and swung it as we walked. I hoped to cheer her. But I don't think it did. Me neither.

At supper Annie remarked, "What's that color all over your knees?"

I looked down. Oh my God. The Mess's pancake make-up she gave us for our legs. "I fell in the mud."

"Mud?" She took a swipe at my knees. "This isn't the color of any mud I've seen. It looks like Bess's makeup."

"It's mud, leave me alone."

"What did you do, rob a bank?" She smiled at me, not her old I'm-glad-I-caught-you smile, but like we were in cahoots, on the same rung climbing into adulthood.

I was thrilled to death. But then she let her bang fall over half her face, like dropping a curtain over her private room.

CHAPTER 24

To comfort ourselves Glorybe, the Mess, Selina and I climbed to the top of the bleachers in our church gym, waiting for the square dance to begin and waiting desperately to get a glimpse of Gordon Knight.

Usually Glorybe's daddy would have been there, doing sort of Indian style square dancing. The music was already pouring out, Minnie Howard on the fiddle and Chad Tosca on the piano and old Crawford singing out the squares with his gravelly voice.

I wasn't so afraid for Jeremiah anymore. A week had gone by, nothing bad seemed to be happening. And The Indian wasn't worse. The Johnsons were the only Colored people there, but nobody minded.

Selina said, "I bet Gordon Knight isn't even going to show up,"

"Don't worry," I said.

Right now I couldn't look at Dad; he had on a really loud tie with flowers. When I complained he just smiled and said, "Can't your old daddy get jazzed up now and then?" Rarely was he that unpredictable.

Mom was cruising about, chatting. Eliah was standing around with a bunch of white boys he knew from school. He looked so good. He wasn't biting his nails any more. Easter stayed home, saying she wanted the quiet.

Crawford asked us to form the squares. But Jeremiah couldn't dance worth a darn. Eliah and Selina and I tried to teach him to swing properly, putting our foot tight against his and showing him how you swivel round and round with your other foot, hardly lifting it, but our teaching didn't work. He jerked and jabbed at the floor, like the way he cuts our hedge.

"Keep it smooth, smooth, smooth, Dad," Eliah said with irritation.

Glorybe and Selina went into reels of laughter. l

"*Oh them Golden gates,*" and "*the old Grey Mare, she ain't what she used to be.*" We danced and when we stopped I noticed the mayor and the stupid detective, Leonardo standing around watching.

We had a break then.

"Is that him?" Glorybe asked.

"Where, where?"

"Holding your sister's hand."

His photograph hadn't shown that he was that good looking. Those big lips could kiss you way past your own lips, like Colored kids. "It would make kissing more than kissing, like eating and kissing both at once," Bess-The-Mess said. His hair was blue-black and he had slim cowboy hips. But he was no taller than Annie.

"What do you think?" I asked them.

Selina said, "Why does he keep his head to one side?"

"He's got only one good eye."

"Wow, that's neat," The Mess said. The music was going again and the whole gym was packed with old fogies and teenagers and parents and some little kids dancing with their parents and Mom and Dad down there too.

"What are they doing here?" I nodded toward the mayor and the stupid detective Leonardo standing next to the mayor. They were staring at Jeremiah.

"Who are they?" Glorybe asked.

"Mayor Cornell, you know that awful Leland's father and his friend, awful detective, Leonardo," Selina said.

But we didn't watch them anymore because Annie was forming a square far away. She didn't want to be anywhere near us and I knew she hoped I wouldn't say, *hi*, which of course I did, waving away, sort of blinking my eyes and jumping up and down. But guess what, she pretended she didn't see me. I thought I looked pretty good, with my braids out and wearing her old dirndl skirt.

Annie was dressed in a yellow broomstick skirt with tiny white daisies. She had twisted it over and over on Suzy's broom and Suzy complained all over the place that she couldn't work, which of course made her happy as a clam. When Annie undid the skirt, rows of little pleats, like tightly plowed fields, burst out. On the sleeve of her blouse, that some missionary had brought her from Mexico, were dangling red string ties that danced with exuberance when she moved. Her long bang hid half her face, smooth as a silk scarf.

Gordon Knight's bad eye was closed as if he were permanently winking, permanently flirting. To see Annie with his good eye he had this fetching way of rolling his head back and off to the side, like he was totally entranced and drunk with love, like he was throwing his head back to hear the music, as if the music were coming from her. And her head was to the other side, looking at him with her one exposed eye. I smiled to myself thinking what a perfect match they were, him with one blind eye from birth and her with one blind eye from hair.

"Swing your partner," Old Crawford graveled out. He seemed to be calling just for Annie and Gordon, lilting his words toward them, clapping his hands and the rest of us began to clap all around and sway and swing and Jeremiah having the best time, his skinny shoulders heaving to the sound of the piano and Minnie Howard's sour notes on the violin.

They moved as one person, Annie and Gordon. She had hold of his left forearm muscle exactly where his white shirtsleeve was rolled tight above it. Their faces were flushed and ecstatic and she let her lips slowly open, just a little. I wished I was her. They swung as if air was blowing up under their feet. They swung like there was no floor and no people and no end to anything.

The music stopped. It was intermission. It didn't matter. Annie and Gordon were making their own whirling music, like those wonderful whirling moments in my kayak or up in the tower with the pigeons, like nothing else mattered.

Still they danced even though the people began to move toward the refreshment table. But Annie and Gordon spun on and on until many stopped where they were going and watched. People started clapping to the rhythm of their dancing. Only then did Gordon and Annie come to, like out of a dream, and smile all around to everyone. I never saw such a smile on Annie.

My attention was then pulled toward the end of the gym. I noticed Jeremiah headed for the desserts when the two vultures, the mayor and the detective surrounded him.

I was really frightened after that fight Leland had with Eliah.

I remembered Strickland had called Leland, to his face, a no good bum and told him not to come near his daughter again. But Mom said that the mayor hid facts in order to save his son.

The mayor and Leonardo pointed to the outside door of the gym. Jeremiah followed them. I grabbed Selina to go with me. Glorybe was in the bathroom, the Mess with her. I thought of getting Mom and Dad but they were way at the opposite end welcoming some new parishioners.

Selina and I hid in the forsythia bushes to see where they were taking Jeremiah. They stopped on the lawn of our manse.

The detective was saying "...and where do you come from? Nigeria or what's that other place, the Congo?"

"You know I don't."

"But you're blacker than a moonless night. Where did you come from?" he asked again. "We want to put it in the record."

The mayor turned on him, "This is not helpful questioning."

Leonardo grinned.

"I'll get right to the point. You have a knife?" the mayor asked.

"What do you want to know for?"

"Could you just answer the question."

"I...do."

"What do you have a knife for?"

"For fishing."

"So you go down in the river a lot."

Jeremiah didn't answer.

"Answer, please," The mayor, said, gruffly.

"Why are you asking me?"

"Because I want to," The Mayor said. He seemed more enormous than ever but with bent shoulders. Leland looked like him, big jaws and thin forehead.

"We want to talk about your record," Leonardo said.

"What record is that you're talking about?"

"Your record, mister," Leonardo said.

"I don't have a record," Jeremiah said.

"You been in fights." The mayor said.

I felt like saying what about your own kids. I'd seen them kick that Dominick kid, like they wanted to kill him and then how they accosted Eliah.

"Two fights, "Jeremiah said, "I didn't start them. Nobody got hurt in the bar. Nobody was arrested."

The mayor moved toward Jeremiah in a threatening way, close to his face. And Leonardo came in closer too.

Leonardo poked Jeremiah's arm. "But look at them eyes, like where's the white around your eyes. Is it because you walk in that muddy river to fish for them muddy fish and it stays on you?"

The mayor hid a smile. Jeremiah, his hands at his sides were rolled into fists. He moved forward. Was he going to hit the detective?

But just in time the mayor raised his voice. "What's the matter with you, detective? You lost your head? You get out of here, sit in the car."

Leonardo stepped backward almost bumping into us and went to the car on the street, but leaned out the window trying to listen. I'd never heard anybody talk like Leonardo had to Jeremiah, not even in our playground where kids can be mean as snakes.

I wanted to run inside and get my parents. But Selina and I knew we had to stay and listen.

131

The mayor, tucking his finger into his collar said, "I better get down to business. "Would you show me?" He pointed at Jeremiah's belt.

"What do you want?"

"Just to see your knife."

"What for?"

"Please. I just want to take a look."

Jeremiah hesitated and then took the knife off his belt, but held onto it.

"Mother of pearl, huh?" The mayor said. "Could I borrow this?"

"What for?" Jeremiah said.

"We just need to check it out to clear your name."

"Check what out? There wasn't any reason for me to kill Mr. Strickland. I've got to get back inside."

"You're, you know, under suspicion so we'd like to help you clear that up. And Mrs. Strickland told us you asked for a raise in pay and Mr. refused."

"You think I'd kill a man for that?"

"People kill for all kinds of reasons," The mayor said, poking a finger inside his collar again.

His fists at his side, Jeremiah said, "I would never kill anybody. I got Jesus Christ in my heart."

That stupid Leonardo hollered from the car, "What you mean you got Jesus Christ in your heart? He's not yours. You acting like you own him?"

Jeremiah shouted back, "No, I do not. Jesus Christ owns me."

The mayor said again, in an unctuous voice, "If we could just borrow the knife. We'll bring it back tomorrow. I'd like to clear your name, Jeremiah."

Jeremiah looked down at the waiting hand. He looked a while longer. Then a while longer. I held my breath. I hoped he wouldn't hand it over. But he did.

"Don't worry about it. We'll bring it back. Thanks for talking to us, Jeremiah. Sorry to disturb you." The mayor paused, "I would suggest you don't go on any little excursions, until this is all washed away."

CHAPTER 25

$\mathcal{L}$ater that evening I went to sit on the Johnson porch to catch fireflies with Selina when we heard Jeremiah's voice rise. "But they don't scare me. This isn't like the south."

"But why did they want to see it?" Easter asked.

"They asked to."

"But you didn't give it to them? Jeremiah?"

"I lent it to them. They said to clear my name."

"Jeremiah." She rose up as if to run. "You have always been a trusting fool. Now they can claim anything." Selina and I rushed inside. Easter held her head. "How could you do that? Didn't you think? Not to clear your name but so they can accuse you. What were you thinking?"

Nobody talked then. Jeremiah waved his hand. "A lot of nonsense. I'm not going to think about it."

"To save that scum."

"Daddy what are we going to do?" Eliah had come in. They're out to get you because there is no evidence against that Leland. The knife they will claim is the murder knife."

"They railroading you," Easter said, "Maybe both The mayor's sons are guilty."

Jeremiah slumped in his chair. Jeremiah got up off his chair. Easter said, "Oh Lordy. Oh Lordy."

"Dad, they could give you the death penalty. They would say it was premeditated."

Jeremiah punched the air with his fists. "Even if they kill me I won't be dead. I'll be with them day and night eating away at their black hearts. I'll be a worm inside their conscience, forever."

Easter took his head in her hands. "You got to listen to me. You got to roll out from under the crooked engine of justice, roll right out of the way of the steam engine of evil."

"How do you think we're going to do that?" He asked.

"Jeremiah, my breath stops at the stopping of your breath." Easter said. "We take no chances."

"What do you want him to do?" Selina asked. Eliah put his hand on Jeremiah's shoulder. "Those men mean it, Dad."

"The mayor will see to it that you won't go free." Easter took his hand.

"A knife doesn't prove anything," Jeremiah said.

"There is only one thing to do," Easter said.

Selina and I clung to each other shaking, not knowing what they were telling Jeremiah to do.

Jeremiah was pounding up and down the floor. "The north was going to be our north star, navigate us into a sweet harbor filled with golden sunshine."

"But the sun has died and night has fallen on us," Easter said.

Jeremiah took a deep breath. "My father, when I was very young read me from the book of Jeremiah. *"For they shall fight against thee but they shall not prevail. For I stay with you, Jeremiah, saith the Lord."* He looked at all of us and said, "You kids stand up straight through the valley of death. The Lord will be with us."

"There is no wading through this valley, my husband," Easter said. "I'll pack you food."

Jeremiah stamped his foot. "Living is fear and I say to that fear, don't never lie down."

Now Easter was hollering, "You cannot stay here. Giving them your knife was a hanging noose."

Selina and I didn't move.

"I am an innocent man," he shouted back. "Even if they bring boulders down on my head or hang me from a tree I am still an innocent man and God knows that."

"Daddy," Eliah said with anguish, "You've got to. When the law is wrong you got no choice."

"I beg you," Easter said. "You have to think of us, have pity on your children and on me. I want your heart to come back pounding against my heart." She pounded her chest.

"I cannot," Jeremiah said.

"I will carry no lamentations, knowing your foot fall will be going on making prints on this earth wherever you are." Easter enclosed him with her arms.

Then I whispered what nobody had said out loud, "You want Jeremiah to run away."

He turned swiftly toward me. "I'm not a running Nigger."

"Why can't we go with you?" Selina cried out.

"With so many they'd catch us in a minute," Eliah answered.

"Now, tonight," Easter said. "The river washes away the clues." She held him tight. "You must run and run until they forgets, keep running until they forgets who you are, what name you got, what face on you. Just keep on running until you are safe."

Selina threw her arms around him too.

"Jeremiah," I said, "I'm giving you my kayak."

He looked up, taking in my eyes carefully and reached to take my hands. "Your kayak, Theodora?" His eyes looked red, not black. "No. No," he said. "I couldn't. But, thank you, I thank you."

"You have to take it." Tears were pouring out of my eyes so fast I could hardly see.

"No. no, no. I'm not going anywhere. But I thank you. You are a beautiful person.

I didn't want to leave them but I knew my parents would be worried where I was. When I got home and told my parents we all worried through the night for Jeremiah. I'm sure nobody slept.

CHAPTER 26

*E*liah was frantically turning over every rock. My heart was beating fast with hope. We had to find it and save Jeremiah, I kept saying to myself. Last night after I left a stone came flying through their window with a note attached. "You are going where you belong."

The river was low and I thought of the time Eliah had been saved. Saved by Jesus. Maybe, somehow Jesus would save Jeremiah now. I glanced where the spot was down stream from us and where the river grows deeper. That day that Eliah was saved I was with Selina and her family and not Glorybe. The Baptist minister barefoot and in a white silk robe lead Eliah by the hand. Eliah was in a white robe also, looking like a saint, though I wasn't sure what a saint looked like.

In the river the minister took Eliah in his arms and laid him back into the water…all the way, the robe floating to the surface. He pushed Eliah's head under and I let out a gasp. The minister was drowning him. Selina turned around and frowned at me just as Eliah surfaced and the minster blessed him, *May the Lord bless you and keep you and may his face shine upon you and give you peace.* Eliah walked toward us with a calm look of peace that I had never seen after that.

Now anxious and solemn, anxious and careful, he picked up every shiny object and we followed his scrutiny as he glanced and threw back each, in scowling haste. I remembered, *The Lord helps him who helps himself.* I had always loved the river as a sign of freedom but then like a scorned lover I began to hate how it hid its secrets. Where was the killing knife? I could see the terror on Selina's face.

We searched until noon and then Eliah turned without saying a word and started up the bank and toward home. We followed. So sad. So worried.

Late afternoon I knocked on Glorybe's door. No answer. I sneaked inside. There in the gloom was The Indian. I moved silently and close. He was sitting in the chair that Glorybe's brother slept in. He was asleep, breathing softly. I took the one crayfish I had found and laid it on his lap. I sat down on the sinking couch feeling as if it were a sinking boat.

A few minutes later the words came. "Minister's kid, sight for sore eyes. This is the best present I could have." He picked up the crayfish.

Years later I understood that it was he who had given me a present, a life long present, the mystery and fantasy of love.

CHAPTER 27

The next day just as we were about to sit at breakfast Eliah roared in, calling my father. We all rushed to the front hall.

Eliah was falling over his words, "The chief of police...to bring Dad down to headquarters but Dad kept saying I was at Reverend Davis house the night of the murder...that had been here with all of you, all evening. So the chief is bringing him here to ask you, right now if that is true before he takes him down to book him."

We all knew it wasn't true. He was home.

We heard the voices walking up the walk and I knew Dad's principles. He would never lie. He thought of lying as one of the greatest sins. Mom would but they wouldn't ask her and it would do no good to contradict my father anyway. They would know she was lying.

The chief knocked and Dad waited a minute to open the door while Eliah ducked into the kitchen.

"Hello Chief. Hello Jeremiah." Dad tried to sound casual. "What's going on?"

"Could we step in?" the chief said and came in.

"I don't understand. Why is Jeremiah Johnson in handcuffs?" Dad asked.

"We're about to take him down to headquarters and book him."

"What in the world for?"

"Murder. But he says he was at your house the night of the murder. And if you verify that…"

Dad interrupted, didn't even clear his throat, he said loudly, "That is absolutely true. He was here long into the night."

"I see, all evening?"

"Definitely."

"The night of June 24?"

"Yes."

"The night of the murder?"

"Yes, the night of the murder."

Jeremiah was shaking so hard the chief had to work at taking the handcuffs off.

"You're lucky you were here at the Reverend's and lucky he's a white witness," he said to Jeremiah, "Because I know how you Colored like to embellish the truth. I'm glad it was not you though, Jeremiah," the Chief said. " He left, tipping his hat to my father.

We stood in silence for a moment. Then Dad said for Eliah to go get Easter and Selina.

When they came back Dad escorted us all to the back yard, Annie and Suzy too. Dad gathered us close. "You must never talk about what happened here, ever. Do you understand, Theodora and Annie that means not even to Gordon Knight. Do you each understand?" He looked at everyone and we all said, yes.

Suzy brought coffee and muffins out in the yard. Easter was weeping. So of course Dad wept also and then we all were wiping our eyes. We held hands in a ring and Dad said, "May the Lord bless you and keep you. May the sun shine upon you and give you peace."

We all said Amen.

Later I crawled into bed with my parents.
"Dad, I didn't know you could lie."
"In this case would you have lied?"
"Of course."
"But it wasn't easy," Dad said.
"He was right." Mom whispered.

Later Dad explained to me that the chief was not devious, not going to see somebody go to jail, even a Colored man, if he's innocent. "That's why he came here first to see if Jeremiah really had that alibi. They don't even put Colored people on the jury. The jury is all White and that sometimes means little justice."

CHAPTER 28

It was the first cool day. Glorybe could see something was not okay with me. I knew I had a secret from her for the rest of my life. This was hard for me to think about, as if the thin veil that Annie wears to church had been dropped between us. We walked to the river.

"We aren't going to see Eliah much. He'll be across town in school now," Glorybe said.

"But Selina will be in our class. I hate the shift of so much. Why can't everything stay the same?"

We lay still. "The sun isn't very warm now," I said, "I have something to tell you."

"Yeah?"

"How do I put it?"

"Spill it."

"Sometimes what you think is really wrong, is really right."

"Yeah?"

"And sometimes what you think is the worst thing you can do is the best thing you can do."

"Yeah?"

"Stop saying, *yeah.*

"Like what do you mean?"

"Nothing," I said, "Let's walk along the river."

Red and yellow leaves were starting to fall and float in the current and get captured on rocks and then rush forward, suddenly free. I squatted by the water.

"Remember how we waited for rain?" She asked.

"I hate waiting," I answered.

"I want my father to get well," She said.

"Me too."

We sat again to watch the river. She picked up one of the bright red leaves.

Before we lay back on the bank in the sun I placed my hand in the river and whispered in my heart to The Indian, "Don't never lie down."